RONAN

SWAMP

AMULET BOOKS

NEW YORK

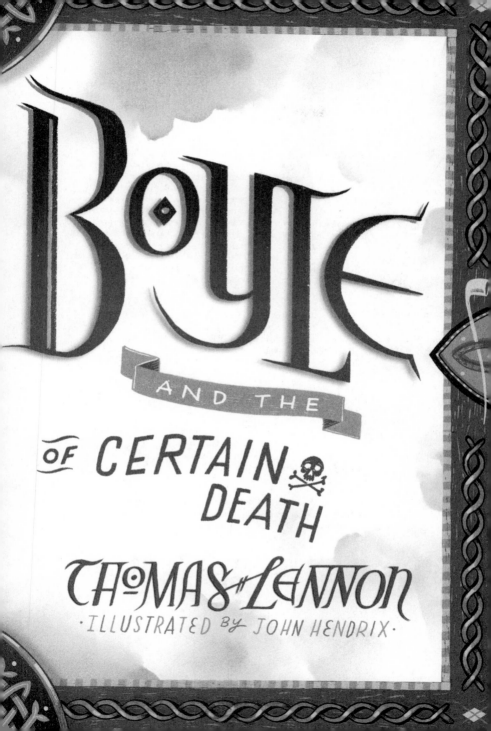

BOYLE

AND THE

OF CERTAIN DEATH

THOMAS LENNON
·ILLUSTRATED BY JOHN HENDRIX·

The Library of Congress has cataloged the hardcover edition as follows:
Names: Lennon, Thomas, 1970– author. | Hendrix, John, 1976– illustrator.
Title: Ronan Boyle and the Swamp of Certain Death / by Thomas Lennon ; illustrated by John Hendrix. Other titles: Swamp of Certain Death
Description: New York : Amulet Books, 2020. | Series: Ronan Boyle ; 2 |
Summary: While on an official mission to rescue his captain, fifteen-year-old Ronan Boyle, detective in the Garda Special Unit that polices the wee folk, also pursues a personal vendetta to capture the Bog Man and prove his parents' innocence.
Identifiers: LCCN 2019033771 (print) | LCCN 2019033772 (ebook) | ISBN 9781419741135 (hardcover) | ISBN 9781683358176 (ebook)
Subjects: CYAC: Police--Fiction. | Fairies--Fiction. | Magic--Fiction. | Adventure and adventurers--Fiction. | Ireland--Fiction.
Classification: LCC PZ7.1.L4492 Rq 2020 (print) | LCC PZ7.1.L4492 (ebook) | DDC [Fic]--dc23

Paperback ISBN 978-1-4197-4701-4

ABRAMS The Art of Books
195 Broadway, New York, NY 10007
abramsbooks.com

For Jenny

Office of Finbar Dowd
Deputy Commissioner
Special Unit of Tir Na Nog
Collins House, Killarney
Kerry, Ireland

4 March

To: Trainees of the Special Unit
From: Office of the Deputy Commissioner

SOMEWHAT CLASSIFIED

Per Ireland's 1997 Freedom of Information Act, I am "delighted" and required to disclose this second volume of the diaries of Lieutenant Ronan Boyle, human of the Special Unit. These journals have been made available despite my own objections and Commissioner McManus himself being oh-so-very annoyed about the whole affair.

Some of the actions described in this new tome are against the policies of the Special Unit. The name of an undercover operative in Tir Na Nog has been changed to ██ throughout the text, as the creature whose real name is ██████ is still active in dangerous covert operations with the faerie folk both in Tir Na Nog and the human Republic of Ireland.

As you know from the flyer in the ~~entirely safe~~ Collins House lift—Lieutenant Ronan Boyle is either deceased or remarkably missing. Information leading to the safe return of Boyle and/or his belt will be rewarded by the Special Unit. (Please contact Pat Finch with any information, even if he seems standoffish! Despite his face, he's quite lovely, especially if you don't get him started on Roscommon Football Club's lineup this season, as he thinks they are rubbish, even though they've shown a lot of character! On second thought, perhaps contact Sergeant Jeanette O'Brien at the main desk, unless she is in her unpleasant human form.)

Obviously, the reward is slightly less for just Lieutenant Boyle's belt, but we can haggle about these details later.

Your friend when you have literally no one else to turn to,

F.D., D.C.

RONAN BOYLE

AND THE

SWAMP OF CERTAIN DEATH

Chapter One
A RAINY NIGHT IN GALWAY

Be still, my beating heart!" said Dolores Mullen, my unreliable guardian, as she smooched the top of my soggy beret and spun me in the air. "Ya look like a movie star, Ronan!"

Dolores was taking a break from playing her fiddle out on Shop Street. Her face was almost as blue as her asymmetrical punk haircut. She was flush from being out all day in a classic Galway mister-chiller. She squeezed me into a bear hug that left me momentarily drowning in her cozy upper armpit. I cringed, as my entire body was still bruised from my painful run-in with the weegees at Duncannon Fort the night before.

Dolores strapped her fiddle and bow into their ragged case, which is mostly held together with humorous stickers. I could see a bit of plastic shrink-wrap covering a new tattoo etched into her shoulder. The tattoo read DON'T PANIC. I don't always understand Dolores' tattoos, but they're sometimes tributes to books that she loves. It seemed like solid advice. Don't panic. I would try to remember this no matter what, even though wide-eyed panic and self-doubt would be the first two things listed on my Wikipedia entry!

Shop Street in Galway is one of the top eleven most-charming streets in the Republic of Ireland as voted by *Free Irish Hotel Magazine*, which is a solid magazine for the price.

Dolores is a busker, which means that she plays her fiddle for tips from passersby. The buskers who perform on Shop Street rival any other major metropolis in Europe. Shop Street Galway is playing in the Premiere League for

buskers. Dolores makes a tidy income. Her most popular songs are "Girls Just Want to Have Fun" and "Message in a Bottle" by The Police. The latter is nearly impossible to play on the fiddle. The only other busker on Shop Street who gives Dolores a run for her money is The Boy Who Plays a Guitar Like a Hammer Dulcimer with His Bare Fingers. If you've never seen him, it's worth a visit to the west of Ireland just to witness his skill. He's amazing. Also, please don't mention to Dolores that I told you how amazing he is.

I settled in across the table from Dolores, readjusting the salt, pepper, and red chili shakers, as is my nervous habit when I sit down in pizza-themed restaurants.

I was dressed in my Garda Special Unit of Tir Na Nog uniform, which is a dapper rig: boots with knee protectors, shillelagh, camouflage kilt, utility belt, Kevlar-blend jacket, and optional beret. For a fifteen-year-old, I looked pretty sharp, except for my thick prescription glasses, which I am completely dependent on.

I unbuttoned my jacket and a bit of steam wafted up from inside and fogged my glasses. We had ducked out of

the rain and into my favorite pizzeria in Galway, which is called Dough Bros.

"Detective!" I whispered to Dolores. "I was promoted just last night. Detective Ronan Boyle!"

"Detective!? That's my lad! Does it come with a raise in pay?"

"Oh. Um. I . . . I don't think so? I didn't think to ask," I replied. "In fact, I still owe the Supply and Weapons Department eighty euros for this new outfit. Plus forty-five euros for the old trainee jumpsuit, and a bit for the shenanogram, plus a fee for the belt and the optional beret. And the trainee manual."

Adding it up, my short career in the Garda Special Unit of Tir Na Nog had left me almost five hundred euros in debt.

"Oh. Either way. You look smashing, Ronan, so very grown up!" said Dolores as she held my face in her ice-cold hands that smelled faintly of rosin. "Pizza is on me, luv!"

And with that, Dolores pulled a crumpled roll of five-euro notes from her fiddle case, saying, "And put the rest toward paying off this dashing uniform!"

She slipped the stack of euros into my sporran* and snapped it closed.

"Bless you, Dolores. This could be my last hot human meal for a bit. I'm off this very night," I said with a nervous whisper, ". . . off to *you know where*."

"TO TIR NA NOG!!! LAND OF THE FAERIE FOLK!?! AFTER LORD DESMOND DOOLEY AND THE YUCKY RED-EYED LEPRECHAUN WOMAN!?!?" shrieked Dolores with giddy glee, bumping the crushed pepper and forcing me to reset the condiments again.

"SHHHH. All that bit's classified, Dolores," I whispered, trying not to draw any more attention to us. "Top secret. But off the record, yes, that's precisely what I'm supposed to be doing. I don't know why they're sending me. I'm not remotely qualified."

"How did they pick you?" asked Dolores, concerned, and quietly confirming the sick feeling in my stomach that I had no business going on this mission.

"Well, I—I insisted, actually. In a moment of absolute

---

* The pouch worn with a kilt.

insane bravado. I told the commissioner himself that it *had* to be me. Why would I do that? Am I a complete eejit?"

"No. Because you are brave and loyal. *Brave and loyal Ronan Boyle*; it even rhymes, luv."

"But I'm neither, I can assure you, Dolores," I said.

In truth, I had just ordered the margherita pizza because I was frightened that I was likely allergic to almost every other pizza combination on the excellent Dough Bros menu.

Ronan Boyle is the opposite of brave—he is afraid of pizza.

Ninety-nine percent of my days are spent worrying about things I've just said to people and wishing I would have said something else. Or wishing I had said nothing at all. I hope you don't know this feeling, as it can be all-consuming. Sometimes I wake up worried about something I said YEARS AGO.

Then there are regrettable high fives that I have tried to perform, without thinking. One of these was with Yogi Hansra, who is both an amazing yoga teacher and probably the human world's best shillelagh fighter. Once at the

end of a class I raised my hand for a high five and said: "*Yaaassss girl.*"

I have thought about this awkward moment literally thousands of times. *WHY?* Why would I do that? Likely it would be the thing that passed through my mind at the moment of my death. *Yaaassss girl?* This is not something that can come out of my mouth without a crash-landing that kills many innocent bystanders.

I fixed the arrangement of the pizza condiments, suddenly sweaty. Maybe it wasn't too late for me to back out of this mission. There were dozens of qualified Special Unit officers who should be sent after the captain and Lily the wolfhound. And wouldn't my personal stake in the case be an additional weakness? I should go back to the commissioner and tell him how unqualified I am and that my personal stake in the case will cause me to make bad decisions. And maybe tell him about the feeling in my stomach.

Maybe don't tell him about the stomach part. Certainly don't tell him that even the imaginary Dame Judi Dench

in my head was worried that I wouldn't survive. Best not to mention imaginary Dame Judi at all. Don't want to "sound" crazy. *Wait, am I crazy? Why am I so sweaty? Is this the right arrangement of the pizza condiments? Why did I try to high-five Yogi Hansra that one time?*

It occurred to me: If I were to back out of the mission, I might have to return the beret.

I tried to collect myself and keep it together.

The mission was too much for a fifteen-year-old. Lord Desmond Dooley, the man I was after, was a shady art dealer who ran a gallery on Henrietta Street in Dublin. He dealt in stolen Irish antiquities and framed my parents for the theft of an ancient mummy called the Bog Man. Currently my parents were serving three to five years in the Mountjoy Prison, Dublin, for this crime.

Later that very night I was scheduled to depart for Tir Na Nog, the land of the faerie folk, to capture the Bog Man and clear their names (and rescue my captain in the process). These were details that Dolores probably should not have shrieked out in Galway's premiere wood-oven

pizzeria, but it's impossible to stay mad at Dolores Mullen. She is a delight.

"I don't think I'm up for this, Dolores," I said, wishing I could burp away the awful feeling.

"You'll be fine. You can probably do it, Ronan," said Dolores. "Didn't you graduate top in your Special Unit class at Collins House?"

"No," I said. "I got mostly B minuses, except for Tin Whistle for Beginners, in which I got a D, the lowest passing grade."

"Oh," said Dolores, clearly trying to think of something encouraging to say. "But—you're lucky! Think how lucky you are, Ronan! That's . . . something, isn't it?"

"I suppose I am lucky," I said, thinking a dreadful thought that I sometimes ponder: *Was I only in the Special Unit because of my luck? Because I fit through a little hole at Clifden Castle that Captain de Valera had needed me to go through to find a baby? I shouldn't be here. Not Dough Bros pizzeria, I certainly deserved to be there, although I'm not as cool as most of the patrons. On second thought, maybe I don't fit in at Dough Bros?*

Galway is very hip these days. Really I shouldn't be in the Special Unit, one of Northern Europe's most venerated faerie policing forces. I'm just a frightened kid. And why the high five that one time? Where had I even heard "Yaaassss girl" before? Perhaps on the radio? Oh, for a time machine to undo all of this.

This is what it's like to live inside my head. I wouldn't wish it on my worst enemy. The only part of my head I'm really at peace with is the beret.

The waitress set down a margherita pizza between us. Dolores shook hot pepper flakes on only her side, knowing full well that I am allergic.

Or am I just afraid of hot chili peppers? Is my allergy really just psychosomatic, based on my fear? And what about that time that I told Yogi Hansra that her new haircut looked "LEGIT"? WHY WOULD ANYONE DO THAT?

Dolores took a bite of pizza and began to weep. Nobody should take a bite out of a Dough Bros pizza the moment it arrives at the table—it's straight from a nine-hundred–plus–degree oven. Her mouth was going through the experience of a Hawaiian island being born from the seafloor.

Or maybe Dolores wept because she knew what a dreadful legal guardian she had been to me. Dolores is quite popular, and one of the most beautiful fiddle players you will ever meet—I had been left on my own quite a bit ever since I came into her "care." At best I would see her two nights a week. But I was never cross with her about this. In fact I should thank her. If it weren't for Dolores, I would never have learned one of my top Ronan Boyle mantras: *Everyone will let you down some of the time, but only you can let yourself down all of the time.*

When our pizza reached normal Earth temperature, we scarfed it down and caught up on everything we'd missed. Dolores and I walked arm in arm through the drizzle across Eyre Square to the offices of the Galway Garda (the Irish human police force).

Captain Fearnley was in his chairless office, reading a report that seemed to be annoying him a great deal. When he spotted me, he leaped to his feet, his eyes glistening with pride.

Captain Fearnley had been my boss and mentor when I was an intern with the Galway Garda in the evidence department. He brushed the rain off my shoulders and eyed me up and down. I stood between him and Dolores, feeling like I was being bookended by my surrogate parents. Or the actual ceramic bookends I have of my parents' heads.

"Their salad!" he said, almost bursting. Fearnley's country accent is like a jazz concert being played by a jug band of friendly woodland creatures—almost impossible to follow, even for Irish people. In reality he likely said: "There's a lad!"

"Half to freight off dem Colleens wifferswitch," he said, thumping me on the arm.

He may have said "You'll have to fight off the girls"—*Colleens*, in slang—"with a stick," but without a professional linguist, I will never know.

Chapter Two
YUM YUM

At midnight, I lost contact with my foot. My brain was sending messages to wriggle my toes, but the signals dissipated somewhere in the snow. The toes had gone rogue like Tom Cruise in so many wonderful films. This was disconcerting. What if I never felt them again? They had been my toes for fifteen years, and I was sentimentally attached to some of them. Ah well, they were on their own mission now.

And so was I—Ronan Janet Boyle.*

---

* My parents, Brendan and Fiona Boyle, had chosen both a boy name and a girl name for me, and they didn't want to waste the extra one.

I could only suppose it was midnight, as there isn't conventional time in Tir Na Nog, the land of the faerie folk—which includes leprechauns, clurichauns, far darrigs, and all sorts of stinky, biting, nightmarish creatures. Midnight was the time it seemed like to a human, the category of thing that I fall in. Specifically, a gangly, nearsighted, teenage human, and the former owner of a set of working toes.

Within minutes or hours, I would likely perish on the Steeps, which is the way that leprechauns pronounce the name of a mountain range I was climbing called the "Steps." The Steps is a snowy set of jagged peaks that separates the Undernog from the southern portion of Tir Na Nog (see map).

After my meeting with Dolores in Galway in the human Republic of Ireland, I returned by coach to Collins House in Killarney to beg Commissioner McManus to send someone else on this dreadful mission. Perhaps Dermot Lally would go—he's a proper dreamboat. Dermot Lally could probably knock out a mission like this with one eye

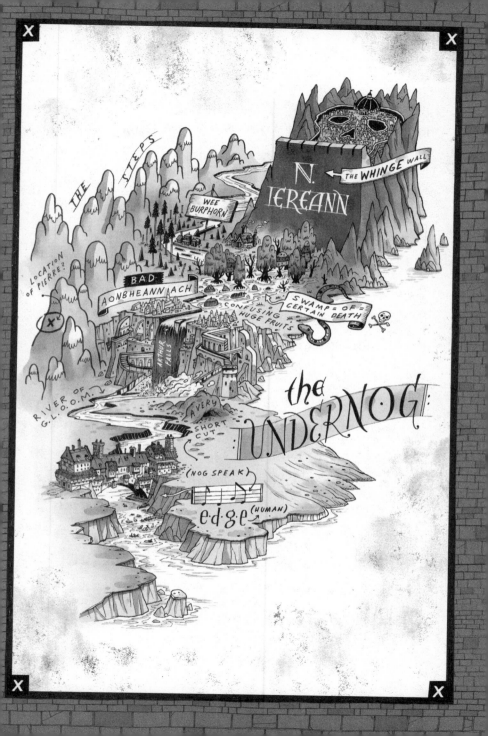

closed—which is how he does everything, as he wears an eye patch over his left eye to correct his vision.

I waited at the door of the commissioner's office, nervously humming Lady Gaga's "Poker Face" and fiddling with the hem of my kilt. As a visual reference: I am as thin as a scarecrow, with a face that is alternately sickly white or neon pink, depending on my level of anxiety. When not flashing neon pink, my face reveals some freckles on the left cheek that someone once pointed out are the pattern of the archipelago called the Maldives. Perhaps these details don't paint me in the most flattering light, but if you are reading my diaries, you must understand that I will not whitewash the facts, *ever!* Unless it is to make certain bits sound a bit more interesting.

A moment later, Sergeant Jeanette O'Brien popped her head out of the commissioner's office. She was currently in the form of a donkey, as she is a púca, which is the type of Irish faerie that can shape-shift into various animal forms.

"What do you want, Boyle? Spit it out!" whinnied Sergeant O'Brien in her classic I-don't-have-time-for-this style.

"I've got to talk to the commissioner, right away," I said, feeling hot and woozy.

"He's in the Netherlands, meeting with the Dutch Gnomepolitz," said Sergeant O'Brien. "He checks his email if it's an emergency. Is it an emergency?"

I thought hard for a moment. My stomach was riding one of the great fictional roller coasters of my mind. Quitting a mission was not the kind of thing I felt comfortable doing over an email. The truth is, I was too frightened to go on the mission, but also FAR too frightened to send that kind of email to the commissioner, who is a serious fellow and in the Netherlands dealing with gnomes.*

So, being too frightened to quit the mission, I just . . . didn't quit the mission.

"May the wind be always at yer back, and may you be in Tir Na Nog before the devil knows yer gone!" said Dermot

---

* Gnomes have been a scourge on European gardens since the creation of the European Union in 1993. Try—*just try*—to grow decent vegetables and not have them turned into little carriages by gnomes. Gnomes are as mischievous as leprechauns, except the gnomes are organized. Very organized. Perhaps because they drink so much less.

Lally, my fellow cadet, and a legitimate dreamboat, as we passed in the bustling first-floor hallway of Collins House. "You got this, little Rick."

For some reason Dermot Lally calls me "little Rick." I do not know why. I have stopped correcting him.

The ghost of Brian Bean (a lovely trainee who died during training and whose specter does celebrity impressions in the halls of Collins House) floated over to me, doing a spot-on version of Flavor Flav, the eccentric rapper from Public Enemy with the clock around his neck.

"Yeeeeeaaaahhh, boy!" said the ghost of Brian Bean. "Flavor Flav ain't going out like that. Where the S1-Ws?!"

"Brilliant, Brian, just brilliant," I said. There was no denying, this was an absolutely perfect Flavor Flav. I think even Flavor Flav himself would agree. But, while Brian's comedy is first rate, it can get monotonous to be haunted by him on a daily basis.

Now, a day later, I was far from Killarney. I would even take a haunting from Brian to be back home in the warmth and safety of Collins House.

My rogue toes and I were crunching our way over the mountains of lower Tir Na Nog, Land of the Faerie Folk.

I squinted up at the summit of the Steps, still two hundred meters above us. It was only visible when the clouds parted, revealing a three-quarter moon that looked like it was frowning sideways at me, as well it should be—this was no laughing matter.

In case you are wondering: Kilts are not ideal for deep snow, even if they look amazing the rest of the time, especially with a jaunty black beret, which I was also wearing.

This trip was not for pleasure—so it might as well be a huge pain. The weegees I was after are the most unscrupulous band of thugs you would ever want to meet. I actually hope that you don't meet them, because they will stab you in the knee and then pour very good mustard in the cut.

The weegees were in league with a disgusting mummy called the Bog Man whom I have sketched below, based on my last sighting of him in Duncannon Fort.

WRINKLES

EMPTY
EYES

CREEPY

SUSPECT #1

"The Bog Man" is what I know him to be called. He may have another name. Once upon a time, I thought that the Bog Man was just a four-thousand-year-old museum piece; an Irish Tutankhamen. The Bog Man is, in fact, a living monster. Alive (undead?), unwell, and up to no good.

The Bog Man's accomplice is a stinky twenty-four-inch-tall leprechaun I call the Red-Eyed Woman with a Nose That Looks Like It Was Put on Upside Down. If you saw her, this name would make perfect sense.

These scoundrels had kidnapped Captain de Valera and the magnificent 180-pound wolfhound named Lily. Lily's fur is a gorgeous rust color and she is one of the best friends

I have ever had. Lily is a lieutenant in the Special Unit's wolfhound division, one of the top three secret canine law enforcement divisions in Northern Europe.

My mission was the safe return of Captain de Valera and Lily to Special Unit Headquarters in Killarney, County Kerry. If I could catch the Bog Man as well, my parents would be exonerated.

There are lots of secret gates from the human Republic into the faerie realm. If you've been to Ireland, you've probably seen them without even noticing. The faerie folk cast small spells to make us not pay any mind to the geataí. I can tell you now, as it's no longer classified: The busiest leprechaun gate into the human realm was a video rental store in Athlone with a huge sign in the window that said: NINETEEN VHS MOVIES FOR A PENNY! NO LATE FEES, EVER– EVER–EVER. PLEASE COME INSIDE RIGHT NOW!

This should have seemed suspicious right off the bat. No human wants that many VHS movies. It's way too many. And the COME INSIDE RIGHT NOW! part feels *very dodgy*. This sign was written by leprechauns.

To get into the land of the faerie folk, I had leaped into a geata with my strapping, slightly insane partner, Log MacDougal. With us was a sleek, 160-pound salt and pepper-colored wolfhound called Rí, who holds the equivalent rank as me—Detective, Wolfhound Special Unit of Tir Na Nog.

The first objective of our mission required that we make contact with an undercover Special Unit operative. He would be awaiting us in the leprechaun town of EDGE.*

The geata we had passed through earlier tonight was located in an overflowing toilet stall at gate B3 in the departures lounge of Ireland's wildly underrated Shannon International Airport. As a result, the trip began with a lot of the standard inconveniences of air-line travel. I had to take Rí outside before we left for a

---

* This is the human way of writing this town's name. On faerie maps it's written in musical notes. E-D-G-E is one of the towns of the Undernog where the language is played on tin whistle. For those of you who play an instrument, the town is played/said like this:

E - D - G - E

walk and a pee. While I was not looking, Log had stolen two dozen Kinder Eggs from the duty-free shop. Before you judge her: Log MacDougal was raised by leprechauns, so stealing, fighting, and making up rhymes is all she knows.

Now as we crunched through the knee-deep snow, Log was in an especially nervous mood. Her low giggle was on a loop. I could sense she was jumpy.

This mission would take us back into her childhood homeland of Tir Na Nog, and she always gets a little itchy when her family is brought up. She kept checking her shillelagh and the weaponized bottle of Coleman's super-hot mustard that she carries on her utility belt.

I was about to collapse from the subzero temperatures and the lack of oxygen content in the air. In the kilt and beret, I was overdressed for the event, while being underdressed for the conditions.

Log MacDougal is over six feet tall. She hoisted me out of the snow and up onto her shoulder.

"Up, macushla, time for burpies!" said Log. She dangled me over her shoulder, giggling like the psychopath that I would think that she is were she not also my closest friend other than Dolores. Log tossed a Kinder Egg into her mouth and chewed it up, toy and all.

"Put me down!" I cried out as my kilt flipped upward, revealing my briefs* to the frowning moon.

Log MacDougal is as strong as three adult chimpanzees. She carried me over her shoulder as if it were ever-so-hilarious. Now I was freezing *and* upside down. My face would soon break the pink-o-meter.

Rí chuckled at the sight of Log carrying me.

"Grrrrrrrr," replied Log, in the language of the animals. Log and Rí conversed with each other for a moment, enjoying a laugh despite our dire situation.

Even though she is a human woman, her faerie upbringing left Log fluent in the language of the animals. Like Italian, fifty percent of the language is naughty expressions.

---

* Generally one does not wear underpants with a kilt, but that is not Ronan Boyle's style! In fact, I was wearing double-underpants, something I do in case of a surprise sheerie flight or kilt malfunction.

My second pair of underpants was now starting to freeze to my first pair of underpants. I made a mental note to triple up the underpants next time, with something from the Thinsulate™ family of products on the bottom layer.

This was becoming a truly regrettable Tuesday evening.

As I often do, I started crying, but the tears froze to my lashes before they could get all the way out. This created an ice-bond between my lashes and my glasses. I could no longer blink.

What happened next was a blur even to Log, who has perfect vision.

"THHIPP!" went something teensie tiny, splitting the air.

My lungs were suddenly filled with the smell of peppermint. Hot peppermint is not delightful when it has been weaponized, as this stuff had been. The burning in my jugular vein spread into my bloodstream. I pulled a tiny wooden dart out of my neck. It smelled so minty.

"Oi, what's that, macushla?" asked Log as another "THHIPP!" cut through the night and a matching dart landed in *her* neck.

Now we were both drowning in peppermint, inside our own cardiovascular systems. Eyes bulging, we gasped for air. Rí had picked up the scent of something moving in the trees and bounded off after it. The last bit I remember was Log falling on top of me, pressing me deep into the snow.

"God, Log is as dense as a gold dog," I mumbled as I passed out. I was dazed, dying, and certain that I had just spoken a palindrome* for the first time in my life.

I awoke sometime later, shivering in a hut, pinned to the wall. I was wrapped up as tightly as a well-made burrito. This was stressful for me, as I have severe claustrophobia.

A torch on the wall cast ghastly shadows about the freezing hut. From the sound of the wind outside, it seemed that we must be still high up in the Steps.

---

* *A palindrome is spelled the same backward and forward, so this is NOT a palindrome, cheers. —Finbar Dowd, Deputy Commissioner, Special Unit of Tir Na Nog.*

I craned my neck to get my bearings. Log was out cold, wrapped in a sack beside me. Rí was nowhere in sight.

"Oi. Psst. Log!" I whispered, "Wake up. Log. Lara. Lara MacDougal, wake up."

No response, even when I used Log's human name of Lara, which she hates. I blew at her eyes as hard as I could, thinking the peppermint residue on my breath would wake her. Eventually, this did the trick. Log fluttered awake, very annoyed. She began struggling against the sack.

"*Muck me clogs!*" shouted Log, using a disgusting bit of leprechaun slang that means "fill my shoes with unicorn poop."

Log flexed, straining against the sack. Who or what had wrapped us in these sacks I did not know, and I wasn't keen to find out.

A tiny nefarious giggle came from the shadows.

"Naughty, naughty! Don't open yet!" hissed a voice that sounded like a Swedish snake. "Don't open them yet! WAIT FOR YUM YUM."

The voice sent chills down my spine, then back up into my beret. It wasn't a human voice, but it wasn't a leprechaun, either.

"SURPRICE!" shrieked a tiny man, no bigger than—and not so different from—a hairless rat. His eyes were black and glassy. His skin was as clear as gelatin, revealing the veins underneath. He had a sharp, pointy nose and no eyelids whatsoever. He had pounced onto the sack that held me, his tiny claws stabbing through the bag and into the top layer of my skin. He wore shredded tights and a hat ringed around with old bells that no longer made a sound.

"Surprice for to see you! SURPRICE FOR ME TO SEE YOU, YUM YUM! LITTLE MIG FIND YOU IN THE SNOW! CATCH THEM WITH MINTIES," giggled the awful little thing.

He leaned in and sniffed my face. His breath reeked of discount rum.

Without pointing fingers at anybody, his accent *seemed* Scandinavian.

"Good sir. We don't want any trouble," I said, recoiling from his rum breath and trying to "normalize the abnormal situation," as we had been trained back at Collins House. "I am Ronan Boyle, detective of the Special Unit, this is my associate, Cadet Log MacDougal. I'm sure we can talk this over. I have many tasty whiskeys and tobacco on my belt, all for you to try, my friend."

"HA. NO! NO WHISKEY FOR MIG!" spat the little man, cursing in what was now *definitely* a Swedish accent. He jumped over to Log's sack like a flying squirrel, the fabric under his arms catching the air. He sniffed Log's face, frantic and excited. I could literally see his heartbeat speed up through his gelatinous skin.

Log, in her wonderful style, tried to bite his head off.

Sadly she missed. This was unfortunate, as she wouldn't get another chance like that.

"NAUGHTY! NAUGHTY KVINNA!" hissed the tiny man into Log's face, revealing rows of piranha teeth. Even Log herself recoiled from the smell of his breath, which is

interesting because Log loves rum and she can pound it like an Admiral Supreme Numero Uno* in the Leprechaun Royal Navy.

"No biting little Mig! Any biting and the mänskligs go into Mig's fine belly! YUM YUM," he cackled as he tapped his belly and scampered off into the shadows.

Log looked to me for help, but this was pointless, as I was also looking to *her* for help. "YUM YUM SOON!" said the rat man from the shadows.

He slammed a door shut and bolted it from the other side.

After a moment, Log said, "He seems nice," because Log is the second-most hilarious person I know, after my guardian Dolores.

"I don't have a plan," I said, "but I know that I don't want to turn into whatever yum yum is."

"I think I can get out of this bag if I really try," said Log, gritting her teeth and flexing her huge upper body. She elbowed and twisted like a musclebound caterpillar in its cocoon. The sack began to split a bit. My guess is that

---

* Lowest Rank of the Leprechaun Navy.

nobody had ever put a human being as strong as Log Mac-Dougal into one of these sacks during their testing phase.

This part took almost seven minutes, which is a detail that I could have left out, but have chosen not to. With a satisfying *rrrrriiipp,* the sack burst, depositing Log to the floor with a wet crunch. She brushed herself off, grabbed the torch off of the wall, and examined my bag—a puzzled look on her face.

"That's creepy," whispered Log, "so creepy."

"Get me out of this sack, quickly," I said, trying not to panic, because when I panic, I often go into a hallucination about my favorite actress, Dame Judi Dench. It's a mental condition that I am cursed with, in addition to several food allergies. And the claustrophobia thing, and some other stuff.

"It's not a sack you're wrapped in, Ronan, it's a stocking. *A Christmas stocking.*"

I did not like this one bit. I started to panic. And then it happened:

I was at the Cannes International Festival du Film with Dame Judi Dench. Dame Judi was doing an interview on the red carpet about the challenges of playing Queen

Victoria, which she has done *twice*. Ah, leave it to Dame Judi to master two different interpretations of a character, two decades apart! The woman is a gem. The jewel in the crown of acting. And I'm standing next to her, and she reaches over and takes a huge sip off of my cola slushy, which is the best kind of slushy. And then she won't stop, and I have to say, "Oi, leave some slushy for the rest of us, you tart!" And we laugh and laugh because we have this kind of fun casual relationship.

"Hush!" whimpered a weak voice from the darkness, bringing me back from the fictional South of France to the cold reality of this dreadful mountain hut. "Hush and be still, beefies!* Don't try to escape. It's pointless. There are too many of these devils. They'll eat you alive, make toys from yer bones. Never seen anything like 'em."

I scanned the darkness for the source of the voice. In the flicker of the torch light I could make out another prisoner pinned in a stocking to the opposite wall. He was the skinniest far darrig I had ever seen. Most far darrigs are

---

* Leprechaun slang for human.

furry red creatures with tusks, but this fellow had been hanging there on the wall for ages, it seemed. His tusks had yellowed, and his pale fur was falling out in patches.

"They're the Free Men of the Pole. *Don't call 'em elves.* They hate that word so much." He gestured with his snout to a pile of human and faerie folk bones lining the floor. "Ate 'em all, they did, while they was still kicking. They like their meat alive."

Log swung the torch in an arc, giving us both a better look at the bones strewn about. The far darrig's voice trembled.

"Don't make a fuss and you'll live. Keep yer head down, play dead. The Free Men of the Pole are not slaves to the Claus anymore, they don't play around."

"Wait. The little monster thing? He's one of . . . *Santa's elves*?" I said.

The far darrig shuddered. "DON'T SAY ELVES—*FREE MEN!* They been hiding out in these mountains for years. They escaped the Claus. Sailed south from the pole, leaving their brothers behind. A clurichaun named Oh So Hilarious Harold helped 'em escape into Tir Na Nog.

Charged 'em a pretty penny, he did. Said he'd ferry them to the Undernog and a new life of freedom. But a big snow came, cut 'em off. Oh So Hilarious Harold fled—abandoning the little men here in the Steps. They got snowed in. It snowed for two human years. The little men went mental. Alone for years. Now the Free Men eat anything that they find; mountain goats, beefies. Even each other, *as long as it's alive.* They say every day is their holiday now that they're free from the clutches of the Claus. I beg you, play dead like ol' Pierre here, and you might just live."

This was a lot of information.

For starters, it turns out this far darrig was named Pierre. I'm glad he told us, as usually you have to guess the names of faerie folk, which takes ages and it didn't seem that we would be alive for all that long. I would have been certain he was exaggerating about the Free Men, except that I was about to find out that, if anything, he was *underselling* the danger of the situation.

From outside the hut came a ruckus and the sound of a bolt sliding open. In a nanosecond, Pierre the far darrig transformed himself into the most plausible corpse you have ever seen. He even started to smell rotten, and I did not know that far darrigs could do things like that. Log took Pierre's cue and collapsed, sticking out her tongue and rolling back her eyes.

Because I am an eejit, I moved a teensy bit slower than those two, leaving me as the only thing in the room that seemed to be alive.

Mig hopped back in. He spotted Log, "dead" on the floor, and went ballistic.

"WHAT HAPPEN TO KVINNA?" he hissed, sniffing her face. "BIG MEAT ON KVINNA! SO MUCH YUM YUM. YUM YUM MUST BE ALIVE!"

Mig picked up a bone from the pile on the floor and poked Log's face. He pulled at her eyelids. He licked his finger and stuck it in her ear, wriggling it around. Log didn't move a muscle. Log is used to playing the leprechaun version of hide-and-seek, which can take months and sometimes involves faking your own death or controlling your heart rate until it is no longer perceivable by others.

"[SWEDISH EXPLETIVE THAT I DIDN'T UNDER-STAND]!" screamed Mig. He threw a bone at Pierre. It bounced directly off of his *open* eye. Wow. Pierre didn't flinch. He'd been playing dead for years and was no amateur.

"One wee mänsklig will have to do. TIME FOR CLAUSMAS! YUM YUM!" shouted Mig, spitting and kicking. Mig climbed up onto my sack with his little cat claws and yanked out the nail that held me to the wall.

I landed right on top of Log, who *still* didn't budge. *She's a genius.* Little Mig dragged me across the hut, and out into the windy night.

I was dragged into a great hall with a roaring fire. The walls were decked out with lots of tinsel. Two dozen rat-sized men were waiting. They cheered when they saw me—bloodlust in their eyes. Then they did one of the most bizarre things I have ever seen. They sang the tune of the old Christmas song "Carol of the Bells," but only used the words "YUM YUM YUM YUM." So it went:

Yum, yum yum yum.

Yum, yum yum yum.

YUM yum yum yum. YUM, yum yum yum

YUM YUM YUM yum yum. YUM YUM yum yum

YUM yum yum yum yum yum YUM yum yum yum.

YUM yum yum yum yum YUM yum yum yum

YUM yum yum yum yum YUM yum yum yum.

(Repeat)

It was very disturbing to have two dozen little translucent rat-men sing this at me. Then they hoisted my sack up and placed me in the center of a long banquet table. They filled their cups with rum. I seemed to be the only major "food" item on the menu, other than a few pass-arounds and starters.

I kicked and flailed, but the stocking holding me was so very tight. So I let out a few of my trademark Ronan Boyle shrieks.

My screams only seemed to make the Free Men more ecstatic. All my kicking and flailing had warmed up the stocking, and from the aroma, I became aware that the stocking was filled with herbs.

I was being seasoned, like chicken in a bag.

"YUM YUM!" they all hissed. "BUT CLAUSMAS FIRST! FIRST CLAUSMAS PRESENTS!"

I trembled in my delicious-smelling stocking. Before they would eat me as their "Clausmas" supper, the little men exchanged presents, which took forever. They passed one another wrapped packages and pulled out macabre toys. The horrific detail of this is that all of the toys were made from bones: A choo choo train that used to be something's ribs. A working jack-in-the-box, which when sprung, popped out an actual leprechaun skull, and a wind chime of what looked like goat femurs.

In every case, with each gift, the Free Men looked . . . very disappointed.

Nobody was getting what they wanted, it seemed. They gave each other fake little smiles with their piranha-like teeth and said things like "ISS PERFFEK" or "ALVAYS VANTED VONE OF THESE," but you could tell from a mile away that these reactions were fake.

Seems "Clausmas" is as much of a letdown for these lit-tle monsters as Christmas can be for humans when they've gotten their hopes up too high.

And the Free Men did this disappointing ritual every. Single. Day.

The Free Men sat around for a bit, annoyed with each other. Someone had made an onion dip that everyone agreed was "NOT SO BVAD." They drank a lot of rum, then gathered around a crystal ball to watch what seemed to me to be some kind of live elf singing competition. A few of the Free Men undid the top of their tights and fell asleep.

Somebody turned off the crystal ball, explaining that "THIS ONE IS REEEPEEET."

Seems they were watching a rerun of a competition they had already seen. There was much cursing. Then out came the knives and time for yum yum.

Little Mig jumped on top of me on the table, and I could see that he was doing the math in his head as to how many pieces I could be cut into.

I would have been more terrified, if not for the fact that I had secret knowledge that the little rat-men did not: Log

MacDougal—brazen psychopath with incredible strength—had only been playing dead in the other hut and was waiting for the right moment to save me with a clever plan!

And boy-o-boy did I hope that plan was coming soonish, because it seems I am also allergic to rosemary, which was seasoning me in this magnificently wrapped stocking.

With a thrilling supernova of splinters, Log's tattooed fist burst through the door of the great hall.

The Free Men screamed and panicked. Keep in mind they had already had a lot of rum, most of the dip, all of the pass-arounds, and many were half out of their tights.

What happened next was not pretty. Log picked up the two closest Free Men and smashed their skulls together. It seemed very unlikely these fellows would ever recover from this.

Log drew her shillelagh and commenced a frenzy of whackery.

Free Men were cracked, bonked, and tossed around the hall. Log's plan was not that clever, just extremely violent. This makes sense, as Log was raised by leprechauns, and is street smart but not book smart, per se.

Log grabbed Mig's knife and slit me out of the stocking. I leaped to my feet, covered in savory herbs. I might have been useful, except that from the tightness in the sack, my lower body had fallen asleep. I was in the "pins and needles" phase. I swung my shillelagh, bonking three of the Free Men by sheer luck as I hit the deck.

Log yanked me by the hooks on my back and pulled me toward the door.

Outside was a white-out level snowstorm, and something I was overjoyed to see: Rí the wolfhound. He was hitched with shredded pieces of stocking to a makeshift sled that Log must have constructed from stray bones.

Log tossed me onto the bone sled and curled up behind me. Rí took off like a wolfhound.

I genuinely thought about going back for Pierre the far darrig but decided to put a pin in this idea for a later date.

The frowning moon was gone behind the clouds. We rode until morning, when we reached the last foothills of the Steps. Now we were properly in what the wee folk call the Undernog.

Rí hopped up into the bone sled and we coasted for the

last few kilometers, Rí keeping us warm with his wonderfully smelly wolfhound body.

When the sled sputtered to a stop at daybreak, we had reached River of GLOOM that flows below the leprechaun hamlet of EDGE.

Chapter Three
OUR MAN IN EDGE

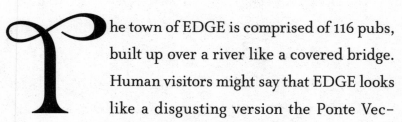he town of EDGE is comprised of 116 pubs, built up over a river like a covered bridge. Human visitors might say that EDGE looks like a disgusting version the Ponte Vecchio in Florence—if the Ponte Vecchio had been built by tiny deranged alcoholics who live for thousands of years. In the center of the bridge is a steam-powered statue of the famous leprechaun queen Moira* with the World's Most Interesting Forehead.

---

* Famous for wanting to turn all humans into sausages and annex Ireland as a suburb of Tir Na Nog. She is *very* popular in Tir Na Nog.

The statue Queen Moira is five times life–sized, stand-ing six feet tall. Her hands are making a filthy leprechaun gesture called "fall down a well." The statue functions like a pointless clock: At random times a whistle blows steam from her bottom, and all of the locals fall down laughing as if it's the funniest thing they've ever seen. Honestly, I found it *mildly amusing at best*, but leprechauns' senses of humor lean toward the depraved.

The rusted tin roof of EDGE blocks out the harsh rays of rainbows that follow all leprechauns, and which can give humans a rainburn if they're not wearing lotion with a she-nanigan protection factor of at least thirty. The roof also holds in the putrid smell of Barfinnaps,* the strongest and most famous of leprechaun purple ales.

It's always drizzling inside the covered city of EDGE

---

* The name is not wordplay, it's the legal warning of the side effects of drinking. Barfinnaps: intense barfing, fitful naps.

because the leprechauns like it like that, and have cast a spell to make it so. Everyone says the permanent mist is great for your skin. This may, in fact, be true, as the leprechauns of EDGE tend to look a thousand or so years younger than, say, those of the entertainment city called Nogbottom. (Although another theory for this is simply that highs and lows of theater life take an undue toll on the Nogbottom folk.)

EDGE was where our mission would truly begin. Along with the captain and Lily, the weegees had a full-grown female harpy* in their possession. They would be hard to miss, but we had to find someone in EDGE who would trust us enough to tell us where they'd gone.

---

* Harpies are giant nasty birds with the faces of dried-up witches. They have a seven-foot wingspan and are absolutely terrifying—*even to each other*. This is interesting, as I don't know any animal of the human realm that is quite so frightened *of each other*. It would be like if sharks ran out of the water whenever they saw a shark. Or if you heard a bear cry out, "Holy moly, a bear! Get me out of here!"

Capturing the Bog Man was a personal vendetta. The recovery of Captain de Valera and Lily was my job. And it was also my other vendetta. So technically I was on two vendetti.*

My orders from Collins House were to make contact with an undercover agent named Horatio Fitzmartin Dromgool, which is a majestic name for the round, gassy weirdo that I would meet an hour later in a leprechaun pub called the Pile of Unicorn Corpses.

Other than Log, I was the tallest thing in the Pile of Unicorn Corpses by three feet. I stood out like a hot pink thumb in a beret. I was starting to get used to the hideous smell of Barfinnaps, which is a game-changing statement.

---

* *Hello, Finbar Dowd here! I've made an effort NOT to interrupt this volume of Ronan Boyle's diaries, but this is not the plural of vendetta. It's really just "vendettas." Vendetti is an Italian company that makes SMALL VENDING MACHINES. Keep in mind that the author of these diaries, Ronan Boyle, was just fifteen years old at the time of this writing, and is still listed as missing in action at the time of this publication. Any information leading to the safe return of Lieutenant Ronan Boyle and/or his belt will be rewarded by the Special Unit, Co. Kerry. Cheers, your associate, Finbar Dowd.*

The leprechauns of EDGE live in the 116 pubs of the bridge. They never go home, and in fact, do not have homes to anyone's knowledge. They nest in little baskets that hang from the ceilings, or the less-organized ones simply pass out on the air hockey tables or under the video poker machines. There's an old expression in the human realm: "You don't have to go home, but you can't stay here"—well, this isn't true in EDGE. Other than hunting unicorns and committing minor crimes in the human Republic of Ireland, EDGE leprechauns live their whole lives in pubs. They get married, make babies, raise children, all in pubs that honestly would get two stars on the human website of Yelp. It also explains why they are so good at darts.

The shrieking of tin whistles in the Pile of Unicorn Corpses was testing my inner ears and very likely giving me vertigo as an unfunny side dish to my serious claustrophobia. Log was sitting on the floor, blowing on her tin whistle with a few locals, and they were all having a grand laugh about something. The wee folk of EDGE were quick to make rude gestures at me, yet they welcomed Log with open

arms. Log can talk a blue streak on tin whistle, while my conversation is awkward at best. Log had bought a round of Barfinnaps for everyone, and they were still in the happy prebarfing phase, all of the wee folks' shoes up on the table to show how fancy they are.

Rí was napping brilliantly at my feet when a fuzzy pig with a hat sidled up next to me at the bar.

"It's cloudy in Killarney they say," whispered the pig. He had rosy cheeks and a likable face that was fixed in a permanent grin.

"Not a good day for flying kites," I replied, speaking in code. This was the secret exchange that we were to say to make sure we were meeting the proper undercover contact. Also, it was provably true; it's almost always cloudy in Killarney.

"Horatio Fitzmartin Dromgool, at your service, Detective Ronan Boyle," whispered the pig, rubbing his pink snout against my shoulder. "Folks call me Figs."

Nobody from the Special Unit had alerted me that my

contact "man" in EDGE was actually a púca, which is a faerie that can shape-shift into a variety of animal forms. Currently, Figs was a little naked pig with a hat. An hour later he would be a mule, also with a hat. Later that evening, he would be a naked little round man, still with hat.*

Figs had the brightest blue eyes of any pig you've ever seen. His crow's-feet connected perfectly to the corners of his mouth. Figs always looks as if he is about to tell you a secret, which he very often is. The fur beneath his snout was twisted up at the ends like a handlebar mustache.

"I've had me snout to the ground, Boyle," said Figs as he stole a random pint of Barfinnaps and a handful of unicorn-and-chips from a nearby table. "The weegees

---

* Púcas have no need for clothing in their animal forms, but as they cannot control their shape-shifting, they are often left in a human state in what we would describe as "naked as a jaybird." This can be *soooooooo* awkward. Later, Figs told me that's why he always keeps the hat handy, to "cover his bits in the in-between phases." Sergeant O'Brien at Collins House is a púca but I had never spent enough time with her to observe this tricky logistical aspect of her fashion life.

passed through EDGE transporting a hideous lady beefie,* a rust-colored hound, and a fighting harpy worth a fine amount of heels."

"How long ago did they pass this way?" I asked, forgetting that there isn't human time in Tir Na Nog and this would be a confusing question to a púca. Figs swiped another beer from a nearby table and guzzled it—as faerie folk love to drink and steal, even when they are undercover and on duty, both of which Figs was at the time. "Never mind, I'd like to get after them as quickly as possible. It's imperative. They could be anywhere. The Strange Place in the Boglands. Up in the Town of Doors. Dun Gollie."†

"Perhaps you can make sense of this," said Figs, handing me a large leaf that had been folded over many times.

---

* By human standards, Captain de Valera is quite striking, with mismatched green and brown eyes, and hair the color of the semiprecious stone called jet. Her face is somewhat hypnotic. This is not my opinion. At least I don't think so. This is an objective fact that the captain is very attractive, just not by leprechaun standards.

† Dun Gollie is the down-noggest city in Tir Na Nog, populated entirely by Gancanaghs, nasty faerie folk so beautiful that a human will fall in love with them upon a single glance.

It was a massive clover leaf. My face beamed as I unfolded it. Etched into the leaf was a riddle in human English.

While it was a wee bit difficult to read, the S's had the distinct loops of the signature of Captain Siobhán de Valera! Riddles are often the official way that Special Unit officers send covert messages to each other. Clearly the captain had scratched this in hopes of getting it into the hands of a Special Unit officer, and now it was! Even if it was just lowly Ronan Boyle!

"Where did you get this?!" I whisper-shrieked, bonking my beret on the roof of the tiny pub.

"I've got rabbits all over the 'nog, one picked up the scent of a Special Unit wolfhound and she found this on their trail, tacked into a massaman tree," said Figs, draining another Barfinnaps. "I've been trying to crack it, but it's a doozy."

The wee folk love rhymes and poems and filthy limericks, but riddles can be like kryptonite to them because they drink way too much and become easily confused,

making even simple riddles seem very complicated to their tiny pickled minds.

Captain de Valera has the highest-level clearance of the Special Unit, so the riddle would be hard to crack, even for me. It reads as follows:

Sometimes I stretch, more oft' I bend,
Sacajawea and Fawcett are friends.
Current runs through me, but no voltage at all.
Into my bed Queen Victoria falls,
I have a few banks, but locks all about
You should know this by now, it's right under your snout.

You've probably already guessed the answer. But I hadn't slept in three days, and had spent the previous evening as almost—yum yum for the Free Men of the Pole. It took me a few moments to howl out:

"RIVER! Victoria is a famous waterfall. Banks, bends, beds, locks—all river things. Sacajawea and Fawcett—river

explorers. They've taken the captain and Lily away on the river!"

"Ah, the River of GLOOM. The worst possible scenario. Probably the most dangerous body of water in Tir Na Nog, after the Floating Lakes and the Stream of Good Whiskey. Horrible creatures in the River of GLOOM. Dangerous currents. Unnavigable falls. We'll almost certainly die," said Figs, matter-of-fact, shoving his nose into another stolen pint of Barfinnapps. And then he added: "We had better leave right away."

The tin whistles stopped. A huge hand landed on Figs's shoulder, then a fist arrived at his snout, delivering a spectacular punch. Figs was about to meet Log MacDougal. It was *her* pint that he had swiped, and boy-o-boy does Log MacDougal love to fight, even more than she hates to have her drink stolen by handsome pigs.

I didn't have time to make introductions.

Glasses shattered. Inexpensive pub furniture went flying. Rí awakened and howled. Log wrestled Figs to the ground, but Horatio Fitzmartin Dromgool is a pretty good fighter himself. He bit Log squarely on the nose and delivered a hard little hoof to her solar plexus. They rolled across a few leprechaun-sized tables, coating themselves in Barfinnaps, their faces stuck with random bits of chips and fried unicorn. I dove in to break up the fight, sending my kilt flying above my head, which would have been more embarrassing had I not been wearing my trademark double underwear.

I hopped up. "Stop it right now!" I screamed in the ever-changing voice of a fifteen-year-old. Then I made a rather big faux pas: I pulled my shillelagh.

The leprechauns had tolerated a beefie in their midst, but only because I had not shown any signs of hostility. A beefie drawing their shillelagh in one of the EDGE bridge pubs is a breach of etiquette. A gasp that could be heard in outer space rippled through the Pile of Unicorn Corpses. Log and Figs stopped fighting and looked at me, their faces mortified, a few wet chips falling off of them. You could cut the tension with a knife. Figs waddled toward me, gesturing for me to remain calm with his hooves.

"Easy big beefie, easy big boy," whispered Figs, looking at me like I was a time bomb, when in fact I was just a very pink Ronan Boyle.

The leprechauns set down their drinks (always a bad sign) and eyed me, readying their tin whistles like switch-blades. I could sense that they were about to pounce. Figs leaned in close to me.

"Sorry Boyle, I'm undercover," he said. "I can't let them know that I'm with you, so make this look like a real fight."

With that, Figs splashed a pint of Barfinnaps in my face and kicked me squarely in the stomach. I'm not sure how I was supposed to make this *look* any more real than it already did, because the kick really hurt. (Pigs have surprisingly hard hooves. Figs's hoof was arguably the only not-mushy thing about him, other than his hat.) Figs bit me on the ear and pulled me toward the door.

"That's right! I said take yer stinking wolfhound and don't come back!" shouted Figs.

This was just for show, as the locals wouldn't under-stand what he said since it was not played on the tin whistle.

Figs gave me a kick in the posterior, and I tumbled out of the pub and into the wet wooden main drag of EDGE. Rí trotted out after me with my beret, which had been knocked off in the "pretend" scuffle.

"Meet me at the boat landing one human hour from now. I can secure us a vessel and a captain," whispered Figs as he slammed the little door to the pub closed behind him.

It was drizzling out on the main drag because it always is. Dazed and battered, I picked myself up and went over to a small fountain to wash the Barfinnaps off my face.

As it turns out, the fountains in EDGE also flow with Barfinnaps, so splashing my face from the fountain only compounded the problem, adding more Barfinnaps to my eyes and nose. YECCCHH.

I quietly barfed, and then pulled out my tin whistle. I consulted my translation book, and then asked a passing wee woman how I might get to the boat landing that Figs had mentioned. She gave me very precise, rude directions, which involved sticking a pickle in my ear until it came out

my nose. It was either a nasty insult or a genuine mistranslation on my part. As I have stated: I am not very good on the tin whistle and received the lowest passing grade in the class at Collins House.

Rí and I made our way through the wooden bridge that is EDGE, passing at least one hundred of the 116 pubs. EDGE leprechauns love a specific kind of harp music that they call heavy metal. It's nothing at all like the human version of heavy metal—leprechaun heavy metal is gentle music about the smelting and handling of precious metals, the heavier, the better. The all-time biggest hit in the leprechaun heavy metal genre is a song called "Girl, Let's Find a Forge and Smelt this Platinum (into Buckles)," and the inappropriate but infectious party jam, "Wee Woman Got Some Brass in Her Pants."

Relaxing heavy metal drifted out of almost every building. The wooden streets of EDGE are consistently creaky—the result of thousands of years of drizzle on raw wood. It's a dangerous combination and the type of thing

that leprechauns couldn't care less about. There was a seventy-five percent chance that Rí and I would fall through the wooden street and into the river far below.

I, Ronan Boyle, can worry about multiple things at the same time, so I also fretted about what would happen to Log without me. Of course, Log can take care of herself. If anything, I should worry what Log was doing to everyone else in the Pile of Unicorn Corpses. Then I worried that Log must be SO WORRIED about me. And rightfully so! I do not instill confidence, except for the beret.

As we tiptoed through town, Rí and I had to pass ever-so-gently over many wee folks who were in the fitful napping phase of their bleak Barfinnaps journey.

"[Something in the language of the animals]?" asked Rí of a stout Yorkshire terrier that trotted by, wearing the standard of the leprechaun royal family. After some indecorous butt sniffing between them, the terrier gave Rí directions to the harbor.

The stout Yorkie's directions led us below town and into

a zigzag of poorly constructed rope bridges. As carefully as we could, we made our way to the harbor below.

As it is covered by an ancient bridge, the EDGE harbor is always pitch dark. As a remedy to this, the leprechauns attempted to light the harbor with a system of oil lamps. But, being thrifty, the leprechauns used the cheapest fish oil available for the lamps. So the lamp system of EDGE harbor doesn't light things very well at all, but on the other hand, it also makes the whole place smell like a legitimately dangerous delicatessen.

EDGE is the last town downstream on the River of GLOOM. River houseboats (the most common vessel on the river) are dismantled in EDGE harbor, where their parts are added to the structure of the town above, mostly in the form of new pubs. (It's cheaper to get a new boat Upnog in Wee Burphorn and float downstream than to spend the fuel to chug up the river against the current.) There were a few ancient-looking vessels moored to the piers, all of which had steam-powered motors, designed to travel Upnog. The

largest of these was a houseboat-type craft. It was a two-story steamer almost three meters tall and fifteen meters long. Wooden letters across the stern spelled out the name, but two significant letters had fallen off. I strongly suspect that at some point the complete letters must have spelled out the name the *Lucky Devil*.

From all the frightening things that were about to transpire for me and my fellow travelers on this ship, the broken name was more fitting. I will always remember the ship as precisely what was written on the stern: *ucky   evil*.

Chapter Four
ANCHORS AWEIGH

curious furry creature sat on the upper deck of the houseboat, puffing on a clay pipe. She was one meter tall and covered head-to-toe in luxurious fur. I had never seen anything quite like her, even in my Irish and Faerie Law class or in the vast tome called *YIKES! A Visual Guide to Wee Folk*. Her eyes were enormous, like a lemur's. Her hands were three sizes too big for her body, with webbing between the digits. Her ears were somehow even larger than her hands. The ears seemed to operate independently and were constantly adjusting themselves. Her toes had suckers on

them, like the tentacles of an octopus. It seemed as if this little creature was built more for swimming than for being on land. As I watched, her foot reached up, pulled her pipe from her mouth, and used the mouthpiece to scratch deep inside her ear. The unfortunate angle from which I saw this event revealed her backside to me, which had markings that looked like another set of eyes.*

The little creature had a broad smile and a way of looking directly into your soul that was either intimate or genuinely disconcerting. She puffed her pipe, and the smoke billowed out of her nose *and* ears.

A wet *thing*—which turned out to be a nose—brushed up against the back of my neck and I shrieked, jumped a foot in the air, and lost five years off of my life.

"Well done, Boyle! You found the harbor. Your friend Log MacDougal is positively hilarious, and I might be in

---

* Many animals in the human world also have this natural defense mechanism, a set of markings that *look* like eyes to ward off predators from behind. Look at the rear end of a *Physalaemus nattereri* frog, for example, and try your best not to scream while doing so—they are the creepiest frogs you've ever seen, especially from behind.

love with her," said a mule in a hat whom I assumed to be Figs Dromgool, having changed his púca form. "Now be a luv and scratch my chin, will ya, Boyle? I've got an itch that's making me bonkers."

I obliged Figs and scratched under his chin. He whinnied in ecstasy and twitched one of his mule legs. Log jogged up behind him, checking over her shoulder and giggling like the psychopath she can sometimes seem to be. Her pockets were full of darts and bar towels. Under Log's arm was a leprechaun-sized video poker machine—all of this was stolen from the Pile of Unicorn Corpses. The poor girl can't help it; stealing is in her blood, as she was raised in Tir Na Nog by leprechauns.

"There she is! The great love of my life!" giggled Figs. Log gave him a playful slap to his hindquarters, and he responded by delivering a spectacular fart in her direction.

Oh, brilliant. Now Log and Figs were best mates. I laughed along, the way that you do when some new person adopts *your* best friend as *their* new best friend, but in reality you're not at all happy about it.

"Have you met Capitaine Hili?" asked mule-form Figs.

"No," I replied, "the only thing around here is that creepy little monster. Don't look right now, or she will know I'm talking about her. She's got another face on her bottom. Truly unsettling."

"Capitaine Hili!" shouted Figs, waving his nose toward the monster with the pipe. He extended a foreleg and bowed, as best as a mule can.

The creature waved back to him and chuckled with the throaty and medically unsound laugh of someone who has been smoking a pipe for hundreds of years.

"*Bonsoir*, Monsieur Dromgool," coughed the furry creature.

"That *is* Capitaine Hili," said Figs. "Say something nice about the eyes on her bottom; she's quite proud of them. Let me negotiate with her. Be a luv and act like a sick little boy; it'll help with the price."

Due to my various food allergies, I basically AM a sick little boy, so this was not too tricky for me.

Figs trotted up the gangplank and had a colorful

conversation with the little captain. There was a good deal of rude gesturing from the furry little woman, and several raspberry sounds from her mouth. Then voices were raised to a boiling point, followed by a flurry of back-and-forth cheek kissing. Figs called out to me.

"Boyle, you and Log get the provisions aboard! We've got ourselves a ship. Also, can you fade me five hundred euros, mate?"

I hoisted the burlap sack of provisions onto my shoulder and fell over—as the sack turned out to be a good deal heavier than I am. We now had a ship and a frightening little creature as our captain. I wrote an official IOU to the wee woman. I was now something like one thousand euros in debt to the Garda Special Unit of Tir Na Nog.

Log hoisted me *and* the sack up with her free arm and carried me aboard. Rí followed behind sniffing the gangplank, checking around for trouble as he always is.

Twenty-ish human minutes later, Log and I were below deck, unpacking the provisions that Figs had brought for the trip. The engine room of the ship is a muggy, clangy, moldy, damp deathtrap. It's also not very nice. This icky steerage hold would also serve as our quarters for the voyage.

Rí napped on a pile of rags near the steam engine. The sack of "provisions" Figs had brought contained coffee, ice cream, *coffee ice cream*, sixteen bottles of Jameson whiskey, a checkerboard, thirty-four tins of Mikey Farrell's Imitation Unicorn Meat, and a copy of the latest weekly edition of *Gadfly!*, the best-selling leprechaun gossip magazine.

A naked little man with a hat over his bits popped in just then from the porthole above our heads.

"'Allo luvs! How's everyone settling in?" asked the little naked man who logically had be Figs, now changed into human form. (Note: The hat was a big clue. Second note: I would later find that human-form Figs and pig-form Figs look exactly alike if I'm not wearing my glasses.)

"Fine," I said, "but we haven't much *human* food in these provisions."

"Keep looking! Way down at the bottom of the sack!" said little naked Figs, "Figs wouldn't forget about you beefies!"

I dug down into the sack, and under several pints of Jameson whiskey–flavored ice cream was human food—eight boxes of Lucky Charms and fourteen tins of SPAM. Figs cackled, thinking this was ever so funny. (The wee folk find it hilarious that there's a leprechaun–themed cereal that humans eat. I did not laugh and tried my best to look annoyed—although, in truth, I love Lucky Charms and would eat it three meals a day if I were allowed. I also am particularly fond of SPAM, which is an underrated spiced meat blend.)

Figs wriggled down the ladder, carefully covering his bits with his hat. He snatched the copy of *Gadfly!* from my hand and a glass jar from inside the sack.

"I'm down to, like, one or two a week," said Figs as he embarrassedly twirled the glass jar in his hand. The label read: OH–SO–VERY HOT PICKLES, NOT FOR MINORS UNDER 300 YEARS.

We all stood quietly for a moment, not addressing the

fact that Figs was stark naked, and perhaps a (recovering?) hot pickle addict. After a while, I broke the silence:

"About Capitaine Hili," I asked, "what, um . . . how shall I put this? What *is* she?"

"Oh, right. You have likely never seen a Tokoloshe in yer life, have ya? Curious furry little things. Don't look at their bottoms. Yech. Like another face."

"What's a *To-ko-loshe*?" asked Log in a nervous giggle.

"The Tokoloshe are river faeries from Africa," said Figs, "but she's a good deal taller than most of 'em and much more agreeable than others I've met. If you've got to travel on water, the Tokoloshe are your best bet—as long as they don't turn invisible on ya. Gotta travel on water with a Tokoloshe. I would no sooner trust a leprechaun to drive a boat than I would trust them to fly an F-16."

"But there's a leprechaun navy, isn't there?" I asked. "Captain de Valera told me about it once."

"Aye, there is. But the leprechaun navy is basically a heavily armed musical theater troupe with one working ship," said Figs. "I saw their musical adaptation of *A*

Bonnet for Bonny Bobby's Buggy last year and it was like—ugh. There's seven days of my life I'll never get back. Anyway, Capitaine Hili is an old friend. The rules with the Tokoloshe are pretty simple: Be nice and she won't eat your goats."

"Eat my goats?" I asked. "Tokoloshes do that?"

"Oh yes. But, hey, *glass houses*, Boyle, we all eat a billy goat here and there," said Figs. "I've got a few frightening shapes that you haven't seen just yet. Also, there's a complicated detail of the Tokoloshe—if they do turn invisible on you, it wipes out their memory completely, so you often have to remind them of a great deal of their biography when they rematerialize. Things like: *how they know you, what they're doing, what a Tokoloshe is, etc.*"

"That sounds tedious," I worried.

"You'll get the hang of it right away. I tend to just give her the headlines, ya know?"

Capitaine Hili waddled over. She had put on a boat captain's hat, flip-flops, and a "funny" T-shirt that read: 2 KIDS IN COLLEGE—WORKING MY FINGERS TO THE *SORBONNE*.

Ugh. If you know much about Ronan Janet Boyle, my

dislike for amusing T-shirts is only rivaled by the fact that puns make me VERY uncomfortable. I'm not entirely sure why, but when people make puns around me, I have the same awful feeling that I get when I see someone drop their ice cream cone on the first lick.

Figs gave a nod. Log and I bowed to Capitaine Hili. I doffed my beret. This pleased the capitaine quite a bit, and she chuckled, with a sound that served as an excellent reminder that smoking a pipe is dangerous and harmful to your vocal cords.

"*Très bien, très bien!*" said Capitaine Hili.

As this was the second thing that she had said in French, I was beginning to wonder if everything she said would be in French. I would test my out theory with:

"*Je m'apelle* Ronan Boyle!" I said, extending my hand and employing my very best middle school French.

"MAGNIFIQUE!" said Capitaine Hili, kissing me firmly on both cheeks and then on the mouth (wha?). The smell of pipe smoke was ghastly. She beamed.

Then she said a paragraph in French that I will not write in this diary, as I could not understand it, except for the last part, which was: *"Ne c'est pas?"** *

"I like zis one. Zee skinny one *avec* zee *chapeau*!" said Hili, squeezing my middle as if to see how long it would take to cook me. "Now zen. Zee ship depart in *dix* minoots!" she called as she climbed the ladder up to the wheelhouse, which was an accomplishment because as she was wearing flip-flops.

"I think she said that the ship departs in *ten* minutes," I said.

"Boyle speaks French! This is a godsend!" said Figs. He leaned in close and added: "Hili and I have been mates for a hundred and seventy-five beefie years, and I seldom know what she's saying." Human-form Figs took his pickles and gossip magazine and headed up toward the deck. "And you

---

* French for *Isn't it so?*

should come topside when we pull out of the harbor, it's a magnificent view." And with that, we got a very un-magnificent view of Figs's human behind as he climbed the ladder. Log giggled, but she does that almost all the time, even if nothing particularly funny is happening.

The ship's engine began to belch and chug. Steam and smoke blasted from a pipe above my head. The whole boat rattled and clanked and groaned. If I were an expert on faerie steam ships—*which I am not*—I would have said that this vessel was unsafe, and "not seaworthy in any obvious way." Many parts of the engine seemed loose, as if they had just been tossed in a pile instead of properly bolted together. Some parts of the motor were taped together with regular human tape. The clear kind, not even duct tape.

Sensing how nervous I was, Log reached out and held my hand, because she's good like that.

A moment later, the ship lurched forward, bumped off the dock, and somehow *did not sink*.

"Anchors aweigh," giggled Log, and we climbed up to the main deck of the *ucky   evil*.

Departing EDGE on the Upnog route looks like sailing out of the mouth of a giant wooden ogre. The rainbows that blast down onto the tin roof of EDGE refract out from it like a prism, breaking apart into primary colors and blasting single-color rays all directions. In some spots, the rays were burning holes* in the landscape around it.

I pulled some shenanigan protector spray from my belt and gave my face a light misting. I offered some to Log, but she declined. Log favors the outdoorsy look of a bit of a rainburn, and honestly, it suits her face, with her fascinating broken nose.

The smell of Barfinnaps began to dissipate, which was a great relief. I would not miss it.

Capitaine Hili was in the wheelhouse, at the helm. Her webbed hand was forcing the throttle to its maximum setting.

The engine of the *ucky evil* thumped and chugged, making a pleasant sound that would become the background

---

* Left to burn long enough in one spot, a rainbow will burn a geata from Tir Na Nog into the human realm.

to our journey and also sounded eerily reminiscent of the 1990s hip-hop song "Whoomp! (There It Is)."

"Zee River *de* GLOOM," called out Capitaine Hili, pointing her octopus finger, her lemur eyes fixed on the river ahead, "*ne pas de* safe. *Ne pas de* safe," she added to herself as she opened a lockbox and pulled out a belt loaded with dangerous items. She clicked the belt around her middle. My bit of French knew that *ne pas de* safe meant: *not safe*, as *ne pas* always means *nope*.

Among the armory on Hili's belt I noticed a double-barreled harploon, a few regular sticks of dynamite, and a gorgeous mahogany club like a shillelagh, only much smoother and with a perfectly round head. Capitaine Hili caught my eyes coveting her shillelagh.

"You like zis, oui?" laughed Hili, pulling out the club and giving it a very nimble spin.

The balance of the club was magnificent. I wished that Yogi Hansra were there to see it. She adored stuff like that and would positively have loved to whack somebody across the noggin with one of them.

"C'est un rungu!" said Hili. "Rungu is African shille-lagh. From the Maasai. *Bon* for whack. *Tres bon* for throw." She mimed throwing the rungu, then made a little gesture as if the head of the imaginary thing she'd just thrown it at had exploded.

I got the picture. Don't get in the path of Capitaine Hili's rungu. Heads get exploded. A throwable shille-lagh that makes things explode—*brilliant*. I made a mental note to get a photo of it to show to the Supply and Weapons Department back at Collins House. If you haven't seen one, here's what a rungu looks like, compared to a shillelagh:

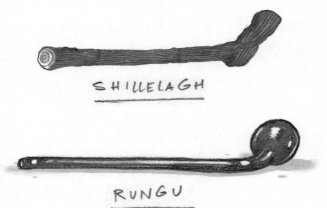

SHILLELAGH

RUNGU

I scanned the river ahead. It was as black as oil, but with the rainbow beams behind us reflected on it, it was not actually that gloomy in the human sense of the word. The name of the river is an acronym, like RADAR. The river was discovered by five clurichauns in the year (humans would call) 2000 BCE. The initials in the name memorialize the wee explorers who were the first living things to fall into the river:

GREG WITH THE KNEES OF A GODDESS,
LYDIA WHOSE RUMP SMELLS LIKE GARDENIAS,
ODIN WHO COULD BE A HAND MODEL,
OSCAR WHOSE BEARD WROTE AN AUTOBIOGRAPHY,
MAEVE WHO IS THE FAIREST OF HER NINE SISTERS EVEN
    THOUGH TWO OF THEM ARE REAL LOOKERS.

Hence, the name of the River: GLOOM.

Ten seconds after falling into the river and agreeing on the moniker, the members of the expedition perished from drowning in that same river they had just named.

This aspect of the story is a bit gloomy. The wee folks' shoes are far too heavy for swimming.

The banks of the River of GLOOM are a dense jungle of Kissing Colleen plants (they bite), young massaman trees, and oceans of giant clover. Clover can grow like bamboo in the Undernog, with leaves up to three meters wide. When the sun is out you can quite literally watch it grow. And where there's clover, there's sure to be unicorns nearby, as it's one of their primary food sources other than leprechaun meat. The sun was beginning to set behind the Steps mountain range to our left, which we had crossed last night in such peril.

I looked up at the jagged peaks and thought about Pierre the far darrig, still hanging to the wall up there, playing dead. I made a mental note to go back and rescue him at some point, but this idea would have to be tabled for a later date—as *three* vendetti at once would be too much for a fifteen-year-old in a kilt to handle.

My eyelids fluttered. A feature-length yawn passed over my face. I had been awake for days, seasoned by elves, and kicked in the gut by my new friend Figs. I rubbed the spot in my belly where his hoof had connected; it was certain to be a bruise tomorrow.

"Get some rest, Boyle," said Figs. "C'mon, I'll head below, too. I'm spent. Plus there's nothing much to see on the river until we get to the falls at Bad Aonbheannach, which is the only place the weegees could have made landing. I've got a second cousin who lives there. He's got a right powerful nose. Hopefully we haven't lost the scent of your mates."

I nodded, half-asleep already, and followed human-form Figs into the hold of the ship. Figs had the distinct smell of a hot pickle on his breath. Log and Rí followed us—Log carrying Rí because ladders are kryptonite to wolfhounds. They chatted about something in the language of the animals, which always makes me feel sad and left out.

Log and Rí snuggled near the taped-together steam engine, drifting off to sleep.

Exhausted as I was, I could not rest. I was worried sick about Lily and Captain de Valera. They are two of the most resourceful members of the Special Unit, but the weegees are unscrupulous and nasty. It was more than likely that my friends were being treated horribly. I wished that this broken boat could speed up and race me to them, but we were at full throttle, and some tape was already falling off of the engine.

I pulled some old burlap together to make a bed. I sensed that Figs was lingering with something on his mind. He seemed exceptionally nervous, letting off a bit of pickle-toots. Behind him, the engine belched: *Whoomp, there it is!*

"Is something wrong, Figs?" I asked. "You look troubled."

"I just . . . I wasn't being completely honest when I said one pickle a week. It's a bit more than that. The stress of being undercover, and all. The double life I lead. Then, as a púca, with all the shape-shifting, it's like an octuple life," said Figs with a furrow in his brow. "I have to tell you something, but I wanted to wait until we were on the river. Away from EDGE. I wanted to wait until I knew you wouldn't go back."

That hung in the air for a moment. Figs was acting so mysterious. I felt queasy.

Whoomp, there it is! Whoomp, there it is!

"It's about your human parents," said Figs. "I got a wire from Collins House just before you arrived in EDGE."

"Mum and Da? Has something happened to them, Figs?"

"Just promise me you'll stick with me. No matter what, we'll finish this mission, and rescue Captain de Valera and Lily. That's the mission. I shouldn't even tell you. It will just be a distraction," he said, twirling his hat in his hand, revealing his utter nakedness, which I managed to keep out of my line of vision by taking off my beret and blocking the view. Now we were both twirling our headgear nervously in front of us.

"Of course we'll finish the mission, Figs," I said firmly, "but if something's wrong with Mum and Da, I need to know. They've suffered so much already. They're museum people—not meant for prison life. They did nothing wrong and Lord Desmond Dooley framed them."

"Well, it's this," said Figs as he pulled a small telegram from his hat. I peeked over the top of my own hat. Upside down, I could make out the name Finbar Dowd, the deputy

commissioner, whose face I could never remember even if you gave me a million euros.

Figs read the note.

"At approximately 3:00 A.M. yesterday morning, Brendan and Fiona Boyle, along with their accomplices of the Kinahan and Hutch gangs, escaped from the Mountjoy Prison, Dublin. The escape was clever, lacking the telltale traits of the gangs, but pointing toward a ringleader with a PhD. Ceramic heads were left in bunks. Whereabouts of Boyles, Kinahans, Hutches, currently unknown. Alert Detective Ronan Boyle that he is wanted for questioning by the Dublin Garda upon his return to the human Republic of Ireland. If Boyle tries to flee, you may arrest and detain him until he can be questioned by human authorities."

My mouth hung slack. Mum and Da—escaped? *Arrest and detain me?* And then I passed out.

Whoomp, there it was.

Chapter Five
BAD AONBHEANNACH

s Irish words go, *aonbheannach* is not all that hard to say. It sounds exactly like as it appears. *A-on-bhean-nach*. It means unicorn. When you see that word, say "unicorn" in your head. There, now you speak some Irish!

Bad Aonbheannach is one of the famous unicorn resort towns of the Undernog.* Bad Aonbheannach has a full-time population of about nine hundred unicorns. Many of those are in the service industries—waitresses, musicians,

---

* *Bad* is the human German word for *spa*, and unicorns like to sound fancy, which makes the name translate as: *Unicorn Spa.*

nightclub singers, celebrity unicorn impersonators, etc. In the high season, the population swells to over three thousand. Bad Aonbheannach is situated right at a spot where a Tir Na Nog's record-holding waterfall breaks up the River of GLOOM. The falls is called Arthur because he was the first thing to fall over them.

We were about to hit Bad Aonbheannach in the height of the unicorn tourist season.

At Bad Aonbheannach, the River of GLOOM cannot be navigated by boats (Arthur is eighty meters straight up). An ingenious system of locks and dams elevates boats through the resort town and into the upper portion of the river.

I awoke with a start in the engine room of the *ucky evil*. Log was snuggling me, her arms wrapped around me like two anacondas in the first bloom of love. Rí was sleeping on top of her, which meant I had over 130 kilograms of hot, smelly, living things squishing me. I wondered if I had dreamed the terrible news about my parents' escape from prison. The engine had stopped.

Whoomp, there it was not.

Pig-form Figs was sniffing my face.

"Oi, you're awake. We're at the first lock of Bad Aonbheannach," he said. "What I was hoping would not happen—*has* happened. Our boat has been selected for . . ." His eyes tightened. ". . . additional screening."

I fumbled around for my glasses.

"You can't help your folks right now, so try not to worry about them. And remember, I'm supposed to arrest you if you run," said Figs, nudging Log. "Wake up, you lot! Additional screening. We must present ourselves to the unicorns! Don't worry, Ronan, this is just protocol, then I'll find my cousin and we'll be back on the hunt!"

I tried to wriggle free of my top two pancakes, who were as dense as bags of concrete that would make terrible pancakes. I could hear the thumping of hooves on the deck above and Capitaine Hili cursing in French. Log and Rí shook themselves awake.

"All persons, wee folk, and animals, mythical or *other*, aboard this vessel are to report on deck for additional screening!" called out a voice with a unicorn accent.

With great difficulty, Log, Figs, Rí, and I made it up the ladder to the main deck. The *ucky evil* was idling in the first of a series of locks. The famous waterfall named Arthur was off to the left, creating a delicious purple mist that tasted like Fanta as it drifted down across our ship and obscured much of the town above.

I was the last one up onto the deck. Capitaine Hili was being interrogated by three medium-sized unicorns (each about eleven hands high). The three unicorns happened to be brown, white, and pink, respectively, which gave them the appearance of Neapolitan ice cream that had gotten out of the box and learned to stand up. Their faces were dour. If you've never seen a very annoyed unicorn before—these would have been three perfect sample cases. *Unicorns don't play around.*

"Are all of these passengers listed in your manifest?" asked the cranky pink unicorn, who seemed to be the proprietor of the voice I'd heard from below.

"*Non*," said Hili. "*J'ai ne pas de manifest.*" Which even in my bad French I could tell you meant that Capitaine Hili

didn't have a manifest. She made a wet raspberry sound to underscore this response, and did a quick flip, flashing the eyes on her bottom at the unicorns.

"Capitaine Hili, you never fail to disappoint. The cost of the water–lift is nine euros, plus a three–euro fine for such an exceptionally rusty boat with a broken name, and the tourists shouldn't have to look at this eyesore," bellowed the pink unicorn. "If you are transporting a weegee, the punishment is death by poking. Plus seven euros peak pricing surcharge for using the water–lift in the tourist season, and twenty-five euros for the mandatory souvenir, of which you can choose the bumper sticker, mouse pad, sun visor, or humorous beach towel."

The brown unicorn gestured with his dowser (which is what they call their horns) to his back, which had a saddle display with a few Bad Aonbheannach souvenirs on it. None of them looked to be worth twenty-five euros. Not even close. And the sun visor was designed so it could only be worn by a unicorn, so—there's *that* little detail. If the beach towel was supposed to be humorous, I guess it wasn't my sense of humor—it said: GETTING BAD TO THE BONE IN BAD AONBHEANNACH! with an image of what looked like a leprechaun skeleton roasting on a spit. (Unicorns hate leprechauns more than anything in the world. And why you would roast a skeleton makes zero sense to me—are you cooking the bones?)

Hili begrudgingly fumbled in her pouch for the euros when the pink unicorn's eyes locked on me. He gasped. He hadn't seen me yet, I suppose. His eyes flashed. He whinnied and reared back onto his hindquarters. The other two joined him, bucking, braying, stomping their huge hooves on the deck. Rí started barking like mad. It was all very noisy and confusing. Mandatory souvenirs tumbled off the back of the brown unicorn, and when they clattered onto the deck, you could tell they DEFINITELY were not worth twenty-five euros from the wispy sounds they made.

"What's happening!?" I asked. Rí put his big smelly body between me and the unicorns, growling. I checked to see if my kilt had blown up, or if there was something out of place that might have offended them.

"To the Cave of Miracles with the devil!" whinnied the white unicorn. "CAVE OF MIRACLES, DEVIL. He shall be a tribute to the Magnificent Equasos!"

Next, there was a scuffle. The angry unicorns seized me, while Hili and Rí tried to pull me free. Figs leaped in to help, but in the stress of the moment, he panicked and accidentally changed into a large fish, with a hat. The hat rolled off his fish head. He flopped on the deck, gasping for air. Log tossed him into the river. Capitaine Hili seemed like she was about to spring into action, but instead she briefly disappeared. A moment later she was back, but couldn't remember whose side she was on in the scuffle, so she cracked me solidly across the beret with her rungu.

In a flash, I was lifted in the teeth of the brown unicorn. Log pulled back her fist to knock his lights out.

"No! Log, no! I'm sure this is a misunderstanding! I'm Detective Ronan Boyle with the Garda Special Unit," I explained to the Neapolitan-colored unicorns. More than anything I did not want Log to start throwing punches, and, as you probably know, unicorn dowsers are as hard

and sharp as diamonds. Three unicorns could easily have turned us into Swiss cheese in the blink of an eye.

The unicorns surrounded me and marched me off of the boat at dowser-point. From the bluffs of the city above, many multicolored unicorns looked down and gasped. It was quite a spectacle.

"He is taken as tribute to Equasos! The rest of you, remain with your vessel, or face a fine of seven hundred euros plus tax and purchase of three additional souvenirs," commanded the white unicorn.

"Don't worry, Ronan! We'll sort this out!" called Log, her voice trembling, not sounding remotely confident that she could sort this out at all.

"*Sacre!* Who are you peoples?!" Capitaine Hili blinked, having lost her entire memory.

The lock and dam system started pumping, and I watched as my stunned friends on the *ucky evil* as it was pumped up and away in the lock, and elevated slowly, not sure when, if ever, I would see them again.

Bad Aonbheannach is the most beautiful place you have ever seen.

"But Detective Ronan Boyle," you say hypothetically, "I've seen the painted ceilings at the Vatican and the Serengeti plain at dusk."

To that I say: (raspberry sound). Neither of those hold a candle to the unicorn spa town of Bad Aonbheannach. The city is white marble, hewn straight from the cliff. Giant stargazer lilies and jasmine grow wild through cracks in the walls and stretch up the cliffside as far as the eye can see. Through a system of aqueducts, the town incorporates the natural waterfall, diverting it into dozens of relaxing baths of various temperatures, in which the unicorns love to float (and pay a small fortune to do so). Some of the baths are salted, for extra density, some are cold to revive the muscles. All of them smell wonderful. There are also mud baths, tubs filled entirely with herbal teas, pools filled

with tiny fish that love to eat the bottom of unicorn hooves, making them feel brand-new. There are also troughs with dye, in which unicorns can dip their dowsers to dye them like Easter eggs. A small fleet of haretrolls had been fitted with baskets and street cleaning brooms, so even in a town with such a considerable unicorn population, you seldom see unicorn poop on the sidewalks. Picture heaven-but-slightly-nicer in your mind, and you've got a good idea of Bad Aonbheannach.

"He's a big walking turnip, this devil here," said pink unicorn, poking me along the most perfect marble street you've ever seen, "a splendid volunteer for Equasos in Cave of the Miracles."

"Aye," replied brown unicorn, sniffing me. "He must be a weakling, as he can't even make much of a musk. He will bow to Equasos!"

The brown unicorn stuck his snout right into my armpit and took a long sniff.

"Not much magic in you, is there, pickletooter!" snorted the white unicorn, giving me a sharp poke right in the

bottom with the tip of his dowser. Even with a Special Unit kilt and double underwear it hurt sooooooo much. It went all the way to the bone of my upper leg.

It was clear that these fellows had mistaken me for their natural enemy: the leprechaun. While I am somewhat thin, and not the tallest person by any means, nobody would ever mistake me for a leprechaun. It's impossible. Not to play into the stereotypes, but leprechauns are disgusting little thieves with filthy beards who smell horrid and will swipe your baby—and those are the nice ones. I, on the other hand, am Ronan Boyle, son of Brendan and Fiona Boyle, curators from the National Museum of Ireland in Dublin. Other than some food allergies, and hot pink cheeks, I am a fairly ordinary human.

"Fellows! Big misunderstanding!" I said as cheerfully as possible. "You seem to think I'm a wee man, but I am actually Ronan Boyle—human of the Special Unit. Oh so very human."

"Ha, the little trickster is three sheets to the wind!" snorted the brown unicorn.

"Typical!" said the pink unicorn, taking a swing at me with his dowser for absolutely no reason whatsoever.

"Seriously, gents, we've all had a laugh, but I'm a regular human here. Never even had a drop of whiskey in my life!" (Unicorns certainly don't love humans by any stretch, but they also don't hunt and eat them as they do leprechauns.)

Brown unicorn gave a sidelong glance at the many flasks of weaponized whiskey around my utility belt. These, of course, are standard issue for the Special Unit—to trick and/ or barter with the wee folk. I should remind you that I was also wearing the full uniform of a Detective Special Unit! This was a preposterous situation. I was starting to hear Dame Judi Dench's voice in my ear, which meant panic time. I reached for my shillelagh, but I realized that the white unicorn had taken it from the hooks on my back, and was now gnawing on it, disgustingly, like a horse's bit.

"Mmmm, a fine leprechaun shillelagh," he mumbled, getting unicorn spit (which has powerful medicinal properties) all over my beautiful fighting stick (which had been

a gift from Captain de Valera and features a carved fist at the head).

"Listen to the walking turnip! 'Big misunderstanding,' he says! Never heard that from a leprechaun before, have you, lads?" The unicorns laughed hard and long. In their defense, I realized I was saying precisely the sort of thing a leprechaun would say. Leprechauns will say anything to escape captivity. This was a Catch-22—the more I protested that I was not a leprechaun, the more I would be doing precisely what a leprechaun would do.

The Neapolitan unicorns led me up the ramps of the city—which, I cannot stress enough, are Gorgeous, capital G. The white marble avenues loop lazily around and through the great falls with a level of feng shui that will knock you on your behind. (The Chinese art of energy balance called feng shui is one of the unicorns' best skills.)

The trio trotted me upward, passing some of the touristy restaurants of the town. Every table was packed, as it was the high season. Most of the outdoor cafes have live bands playing in them. I wish I liked unicorn music more, but it's an acquired taste. Unicorn music is performed on the xylophone, with a special mallet attachment that mounts onto their dowsers. It sounds like what humans would consider "smooth jazz." It can make humans feel like they are about to undergo a dental procedure.

We arrived at a lush tunnel that led into the cliff wall. The only light was from tiny oil lamps that smelled of eucalyptus, which opened up my nasal passages for the first time in weeks. Say what you want about their politics—unicorns know how to live. Their taste is impeccable. The tunnel was wide enough for one unicorn, so I was marched in single file with my captors. A few human minutes later, we entered into the Cave of Miracles, which was not remotely what I expected.

The Cave of Miracles is a majestic showroom. There are burgundy velvet banquettes that can hold up to eight unicorns. Each table has a fondue pot, as unicorns are uniquely suited among the creatures of Tir Na Nog to enjoy dipping foods into cheese with their dowsers and serving them to each other (since, of course, they can't eat the items at the end of their own dowsers).

The far end of the cavern was a stage with a magnificent gold lamé curtain depicting great moments in the unicorn entertainment industry.

Unicorn waitresses and busboys were prepping the tables, folding napkins, and all the thousands of little details that go into running a performance venue. Haretrolls were zipping about, picking up any stray droppings.

A buffet stretched out as far as I could see, which led me to notice the sign above that advertised this place as: THE CAVE OF MIRACLES, HOME OF EQUASOS AND THE BUFFET AS FAR AS YOU CAN SEE.

"You will serve Equasos now. He comes," said the pink unicorn. "Bow before him! Bow before Equasos!"

The unicorns all poked and swung their dowsers at me. A chubby lavender unicorn with a rhinestone-encrusted dowser waddled over to us, puffing on a clover cigarette. His hooves were shellacked with glitter, and he was almost as sweaty as Big Sweaty Jimmy Gibbons.

"Sweet banana-pants, he's perfect! I'm so happy I'm gonna pee!" said the lavender unicorn, trotting in a little dance. He tipped his dowser to me.

"I'm the Magnificent Equasos—I do six shows a day here except on Nonsdays, when I do nine. I wanna eat you up, wee man! I WANT TO EAT YOU UP! YOU'RE PERFECT FOR THE OUTFIT! I'M SO HAPPY, I'M GONNA PEE!"

Equasos giggled hysterically and did let out a bit of pee. A nearby haretroll scampered over and mopped the floor beneath him.

"Oopsie daisey!" giggled Equasos as he licked my face, elated. "I love this little leprechaun guy!"

"Isn't he great?" said the brown unicorn. "Tiny and weak. I want to poke him to death with my dowser!"

"He's one of the best ever! He's gonna crush it. When we put this awful leprechaun in the Box of Death—everyone's gonna pee," said Equasos. "This show just made a HUGE leap forward. This is what I was talking about when I said we had to take things up a notch!"

"We serve Equasos!" said the Neapolitan unicorns in a creepy unison, bowing to him.

"He should have a beard, though! Why no beard on you, wee man?" asked Equasos, giving me an annoyed sidelong glance and ever so slightly scraping my chin with his stubby dowser.

"Yes. Why no beard, walking turnip? Answer to Equasos!" prodded the pink unicorn.

I cleared my throat and stretched to my maximum height.

"Good fellows. As I have very clearly stated—I am Ronan Janet Boyle, human being, employed by the Special Unit, Garda of Tir Na Nog!" I hollered, showing them my BeefCard.*

All of the unicorns examined my BeefCard for a moment, puzzled. Equasos let out an annoyed guttural sound as a haretroll shuffled over and placed a set of bifocals on Equasos's snout.

---

* A card given to Special Unit officers that should grant them amnesty in Tir Na Nog if they are on official business. It states: *Do not kill this daft beefie without a decent reason OR I SHALL BE PEEVED. Very truly yours, Raghnall, King of Tir Na Nog.* Sealed with the royal shoe print.

He scanned me up and down a few times, letting out more displeased grunts from his nostrils. A tiny bit of glitter burst into a cloud with each of Equasos's snorts, because—as I would soon come to learn—glitter is a big part of his life, and once you get glitter on you, it's nearly impossible to get glitter *off* of you.

"Why?!" barked Equasos. "Why must I be surrounded by EEJITS? EEJITS AND NINCOMPOOPS. I AM SUR-ROUNDED BY EEJITS!"

The Neapolitan ice cream–colored unicorns shuffled their hooves, embarrassed. They cast their faces toward the floor as if they were trying to get as small as possible.

"I AM TRYING TO DO SIX AND/OR NINE SHOWS A DAY, AND I'M WORKING WITH PICKLETOOTING EEJITS WHO CAN'T EVEN KIDNAP A PROPER LEP-RECHAUN. IS THAT REALLY SO HARD? TO KIDNAP A DECENT LEPRECHAUN!?"

Equasos's tantrum spiraled into a hurricane of glit-ter and unicorn smells. He used his teeth to yank at the

tablecloth of a nearby banquette, pulling all of the place settings, creating a deluge of glass and silverware. A nearby busboy popped up with a here-we-go-again look on his snout.

"I've been working with this last pickletooting phony for six months! HE'S HORRIBLE. You promised you would do better. We were going to 'take the show up a notch,' weren't we? Honestly, *no offense, Ricky*—you're a good kid, but a TERRIBLE fake leprechaun!" shrieked Equasos as he pointed his dowser at a little far darrig who was poking around at the buffet.

The far darrig's tusks had been blacked out with paint, and the fur around his chin had been dyed orange, to look like a leprechaun beard. He wore glasses with fake human eyes in them, and a tight outfit with shorts made entirely of green sequins that was attempting to be a "showbiz" version of an actual leprechaun outfit. The shoes were gold glitter, and so tacky that any real leprechaun would not be caught dead wearing them. To me, he looked exactly like what he was: a far darrig posing very badly as a leprechaun.

"Our sincere apologies, Master Equasos," said brown unicorn, "we thought this one was better than Ricky, at least."

"Yes, yes! Of course we knew he was a human, but won't he fit in the outfit?" asked the white unicorn, clearly lying and trying to dig himself out of a hole.

The nearby far darrig, who logic implied was named Ricky, munched on a dinner roll, his feelings hurt.

"Oh, he is. By a factor of a zillion—no offense, Ricky, but you're terrible! But don't toot in my face and tell me it's raining cupcakes—this kid is *not* a real leprechaun, just a skinny beefie! But he'll do. RICKY—YOU ARE FIRED. GET OUT OF MY FAT FACE! I NEVER WANT TO SEE YOU AGAIN. GO!"

The far darrig drooped and shuffled away, giving me a very solid nudge as he passed.

"Watch yer back, beefie, and good luck in the Box of Death," whispered Ricky.

"LEAVE THE OUTFIT, RICKY. ARE YOU BRAIN DAMAGED, RICKY?! THE OUTFIT BELONGS TO THE SHOW," said Equasos, swatting at the poor far darrig with his dowser.

The next few moments were interminable. Four adult unicorns and I watched Ricky the far darrig try to wriggle out of the sequin leprechaun outfit, which clearly hadn't fit him properly in a long time. It was an epic struggle. It all felt like watching someone who had been eaten by an anaconda trying to reverse the process. It didn't help that Equasos kept yelling insults at the poor creature.

"I told you to lay off the dinner rolls, Ricky, YOU PICKLETOOTER. *He can't lay off the dinner rolls!* So Ricky stretches out the oufit. YOU'RE THE WORST, RICKY. I hate you sometimes, and YOU OWE ME for the damage to the outfit," shrieked Equasos as he stomped his hooves.

Four human minutes later, Ricky was finally out of the outfit, ashamed, clothed only in his reddish fur (which is what far darrigs usually wear anyway). Then he skulked away. Equasos picked up the sequin outfit with the tip of his dowser and tossed it at me.

"You're up, beefie. You're the new sidekick for the Magnificent Equasos, unicorn of wonders. Lay off the dinner rolls if ya know what's good for you! You're gonna wanna wash that outfit for sure. And somebody get this kid a beard."

Chapter Six
BOX OF DEATH

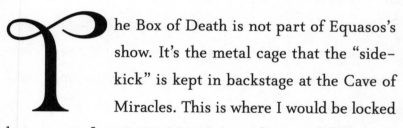he Box of Death is not part of Equasos's show. It's the metal cage that the "side-kick" is kept in backstage at the Cave of Miracles. This is where I would be locked between performances. I was Equasos's new sidekick.

The backstage area at the Cave of Miracles is dim and moldy, and stacked floor to ceiling with magical props, harps, and ten lifetimes worth of cheap show business bric-a-brac. There's a life-sized poster of the Magnificent Equasos when he was *much* younger and thinner. Honestly, from the poster, the unicorn I met was barely recognizable—his eyes had been lifted or tucked or both.

Please note: While a sidekick generally is, say, a friend of the main hero of the story, "sidekick" was an inaccurate description of the job I was now forced into six and/or nine times a day for the Magnificent Equasos. Luckily, I had been confined in the Box of Death with my all-time favorite actress: Dame Judi Dench. As I drifted in and out of sleep, she told me the story of her performance in *Notes on a Scandal*, and of the lasting friendship she formed with her costar Cate Blanchett, my second-favorite actress of all time. Dame Judi and I scarfed down Lion Bars, which she had thoughtfully smuggled in. Lion Bars are nature's perfect candy bar. I had LOTS of questions for Dame Judi—for example, "Was that character based on a real person?"

"It's a hybrid, Ronan Boyle," said Dame Judi, pausing for a thoughtful moment from chewing on a Lion Bar. She wiped the corners of her mouth with an unparalleled level of precision. "Often my performances aren't an impersonation of a single person, but the collection of a lifetime studying the human condition. Do you know what I do when I'm in doubt, Ronan Boyle?"

"No, please tell me, Dame Judi Dench," I pleaded.

"I tell the truth," she said as she crumpled the Lion Bar wrapper and tucked it into her pocket because even imaginary Dame Judi Dench doesn't litter.

Of course she tells the truth. This is the essence of any Dame Judi Dench performance: *honesty*.

A moment later, Ricky the far darrig was spraying me with a hose set to its most robust setting, which I believe is called "jet," but might have a different name to the unicorns.

"Wake up, ya filthy beefie!" shouted Ricky as he blasted me with what might as well have been a bolt of ice-lightning. "You know how they say 'there are no dress rehearsals in life'?"

I nodded, shivering and confused, as I felt like I had heard something along those lines before, perhaps even from the Dame Judi Dench who lives in my mind.

"Well, it's rawmaish! Get yer behind out there for dress rehearsal. Dress rehearsal starts now!" With his little paw he unlatched the Box of Death and blasted me with the hose, using it to force me out onto the stage.

Chapter Seven
BUFFET OF MIRACLES

Like many big stars of the unicorn entertainment circuit, Equasos does not do his
own dress rehearsals. He has a stand-in
unicorn named Nelson who is also the
assistant stage manager of the Cave of Miracles and the
technical director. Nelson works the merchandise table
between shows, selling sun visors and such.

"All right, places please!" announced Nelson, trying
to adjust a headset onto his head with his foreleg. Nelson's
dowser had been snapped off at some point, quite close to
the head, giving him the look of an ordinary horse with a

mustard-colored coat. Nelson has a slight whistle when he speaks, which was pleasant to hear. Nelson had not one but two lazy eyes, each one of which drifted around in its unique orbit, making it impossible to look at him when he's talking, as you will pass out.

A polka-dotted female unicorn in a tutu trotted onstage listlessly. She puffed on a clay pipe and nodded at Nelson.

"'Allo Nancy," said Nelson to the polka-dotted female, then turned just to me. "If any of you don't know me, I'm Nelson Grudgel, assistant manager of the cave. I see we have a new face. We don't have time for chitchat, as we've got nine shows today, so let's get right to it. In the event of a fire, please make sure that Equasos gets to safety even if it means you are burned alive. A few ground rules: Do not look directly at Equasos, ever. Do not *ask* Equasos how he is doing, or if you can get a photo with him. You cannot. Don't bring family or friends to meet Equasos. If Equasos starts a conversation with you, please try to mention that he looks 'great.' Never, ever mention reviews of the show. Mentioning reviews of the show is punishable by death. If

Equasos asks you if you've seen any reviews of the show, you say: 'I haven't seen any, but I hear good things' or 'Everybody loves you, Equasos.' Got it? This is IMPERATIVE. Everybody loves Equasos, and you haven't seen any reviews of the show."

I nodded. The polka-dotted unicorn puffed her pipe, shaking her head, with a smile on her snout.

"Have you seen the latest review, Nelson?" whispered the polka-dotted unicorn (who would turn out to be Nancy, Equasos's onstage love interest, who joined him in a few duets).

Nelson shuddered. "Aye. The one in the *Times*? Brutal."

Nancy giggled, reciting: "*The real miracle in this cave is Equasos still trotting out this out-of-date show that's so full of manure you'll wish you brought a shovel.*"

"Ooof," replied Nelson with a wonderful whistle of his teeth. "Good one. The *Times* always gets it right," said Nelson, turning to me. "You, wee man, if you are ever asked for an interview about Equasos, your answer is: *He's a gem.* Now, WHAT is Equasos, wee man?"

"A gem?" I stammered. I raised my hand to point out that I am NOT a wee man but rather a kidnapped Detective of the Special Unit of Tir Na Nog, carrying a valid Beef–Card and traveling in the Undernog on official vendetti.

"Hold your questions until the end, filthy little wee man, or Ricky hits you with the hose," said Nelson. From the side of the stage, Ricky smiled as he polished his tusks.

Nelson then walked (forced) me through a dry run of the show at half speed. It was a lot of "Walk walk, SCREAM, walk walk, mug to the audience, shake your little fist—SCREAM. Get stabbed in the bottom, SCREAM, fall through trap door, catch fire, look aghast, walk walk, flee . . . SCREAM, flee . . . trap door, etc."

The show itself was a series of upbeat musical numbers (some duets with Nancy, who has a lovely voice), intermixed with minor magic tricks and Equasos stabbing, setting fire to, and generally humiliating his leprechaun sidekick for comic relief. It would be my job to screech, yelp, panic, flail, and look confused.

They had no idea how good I would be at this.

It's like I'd been training my whole life for this job. A big part my routine was falling through trap doors, of which the stage has three. There'd be a snap, and I would drop about a meter below the stage, where Ricky would shove me under the next trap door. Then I would pop up on stage for the subsequent humiliation.

The musical numbers in Equasos's show were on a set list taped to the side of the stage that read:

- Hoofin' It off to Where We Can Kill a Leprechaun for Free
- Girl, Other Unicorns Don't Want Us to Be in Love, but I Will Kill Them and We Will Be Together by the End
- Mister, Don't You Poop on my Haypile, Please
- (Everybody) Get Funky
- Quit Hornin' in, While I Eat this Leprechaun's Face
- Let's All Visit Equasos's Merchandise Table
- Burn, Wee Man, Burn
- I Go Wowsers for Her Dowser
- You and Me and a Clurichaun Corpse Makes Three
- I Gots (the Giggles for Yer Withers)

- Back to the Buffet (Instrumental March)
- (Everybody) Get Funky (Reprise)
- Get out of My Dreams and into This Harness
- Curtain Call
- Mandatory Encore — I Gotta Be Free to Trample These Leprechauns

After dress rehearsal, I was given a handful of damp walnuts and a cup of cloudy water, which was from the famous waterfall named Arthur and was the most refreshing glass of water I've ever had and made me feel alive for perhaps the first time ever?

Ricky the far darrig directed me back into the Box of Death using the ice-cold hose, and after he locked me inside it, I asked him if we could skip the part about the hose next time. Apparently, no. Ricky seemed to thoroughly enjoy the hitting me with the hose part of his new job. I got a few extra blasts for posing the question. Thirteen years in the Box of Death had given Ricky a hard edge.

"I've got a message from your mates," said Ricky,

shaking a folded-up note just out of my reach. "Captain Hili, the gray dog, the giant woman, and the incredibly handsome naked hedgehog with the hat. It's in human, so I don't know what it says."

"Thank heavens! My friends!" I exclaimed. "I'm certain they have a plan to bust me out of here!" I was overjoyed. I also had no idea that far darrigs would consider Figs Dromgool to be "incredibly handsome."

"Ha! Give me five hundred euros, and it's all yours," snickered Ricky, sinister, as he tucked the note into his fur. "Otherwise no touching!"

"FIVE HUNDRED EUROS!?!" I shrieked like the teenage parrot I often sound like. I jumped against the bars of the cage, smacking my glasses into my face. "But I haven't got five hundred euros. I have a shillelagh, three flasks of whiskey, an optional beret, A VALID BEEFCARD, a shenanogram, and a few other precious items on my belt, which was confiscated by the unicorns who look like the flavor of ice cream whose name escapes me!"

"NEAPOLITAN, EEJIT!" cackled Ricky as he shuffled away, still snickering. "No euros, no notesies!"

I was desperate to know what was in that note. I hoped that there was a plan in place to bust me out of this magnificent show cave with a buffet that is one of the great wonders of the world. I hoped the plan would happen quickly, or the trail of Lily and the captain would soon go cold.

The first show of the day was an absolute disaster. I knew my part pretty well, and leaped and screamed at the proper moments, taking the poking like a champ, but Equasos was phoning it in. Nelson the stage manager put much more heart into his dress rehearsal performance than Equasos did in the real show. Equasos lazily trotted from bit to bit, and on many of the duets he did a sort of talking-singing that was designed to save his voice for the next show. This was a nine-show-day. (The good news—the show itself runs only thirty-two human minutes, as time is different to unicorns, and this to them feels like several hours. As the one getting poked and prodded and set briefly on fire—yes, thirty-two

minutes is a long time, I assure you.) The second through seventh shows of the day were somehow even worse. Equasos seemed like he was on sleep medication and slurred most of the words to the songs.

Then, astonishingly, show eight was terrific. I don't know what happened. Equasos suddenly had a spring in his step, a glint in his eye. A whole new level of vim and verve. He must have had a bucket of espresso between sets. He had also fixed his makeup, which can get sloppy and ghoulish at times when he's not keeping an eye on it.

I sat in the Box of Death awaiting the ninth and last show of the day, or the *martini*, as Nelson the stage manager called it. I was down to one damp walnut. My sequin leprechaun outfit was so itchy. Perhaps I should have washed it, as Equasos had said. I thought all of the ice-cold hosings would have helped with that, but they did not. When the outfit dried between shows, it got even crunchier. The fake beard was even worse, as Nancy (who is one of the

nicer unicorns you'll ever meet) had helped apply it to my face with some sort of theatrical spirit gum that stung my cheeks badly.

There was a solid chance that this fake leprechaun beard would never come off. Ever.

I shivered in the box and drifted off, my nose pressed against the Box of Death.

"Ronan. Psst. Wake up, Ronan," said a familiar voice that I couldn't quite place.

I fluttered my eyes and found my glasses. The person who came into view was just about the last person I was ever expecting to see because he's no longer a living person at all.

"Oh, hello Brian," I said to the ghost of Brian Bean. I had always thought that Brian Bean was a poltergeist, trapped in Collins House. Now it seemed he was a regular ghost who could follow me anywhere.

Ugh. Brilliant.

It's not that I have anything against Brian, it's just

the nonstop bits, impressions, and jokes he's always trying out. He would be such a lovely ghost if he could DIAL IT DOWN sometimes. And often the bits are pop culture–related—which are the kind of jokes that don't stand the test of time. (Will a spot-on Cardi B. impression be of use in the distant future? For her sake, I hope so, but as of this writing we cannot know.)

"I've got something to tell you, Ronan!" said Brian, in his vaporous ghost form, checking over his ghost shoulder. "Something quite important."

"Neat, but I'm currently trapped in both a beard and a box, Brian, so hopefully I'll escape, and we'll catch up soon, yes!" I said. "We'll get something on the books!"

"No bits today, Ronan, although I have a nearly perfect David Beckham."

"Okay, fine. Let's hear David Beckham, and just a thought—how about David Beckham working at a McDonald's drive-through? I wonder what that would sound like," I said, indulging the ghost of Brian because he is a lovely ghost.

"No, Ronan. There's no time. I have a message for you, and then I have to get back. It's important. They needed you to know before you get there," said Brian, his face taking on a more serious tone than I had ever seen.

"Who? Who needs me to know?"

"The dead. I go back and forth between our world and theirs," said Brian, a haunted look on his vapor face. "That's where I go when you don't see me."

"The . . . world of the dead?" I asked, suddenly frightened.

"Aye," said Brian. "They actually say I need to think of the world of the dead as my world, too, and that's why I keep coming back and forth, because I can't accept it."

"Oh. Well, I for one always enjoy seeing you in the world of the living, Brian. I was saying that to Log the other day," I bluffed.

"This is important. I've never had something like this from the world of the dead. A message. A specific message for you, Ronan, from some of the old souls."

"For me? A message from the long dead? That seems unlikely."

"They told me, 'You must tell Ronan. Go to

Ronan and tell him: Beware of Crom Cruach,' they said."

"Be *what* of *what–what*?" I stammered.

"*Beware* of *Crom Cruach*," said Brian as his ghost started to fade away.

"BRIAN WAIT! Please stay! I don't know what that means and I'd love to spend more time with you! HOW ABOUT THAT BECKHAM IMPRESSION!"

But he was gone. No beatboxing, no bits. A genuinely mysterious message from the ghost of Brian Bean. I was rattled—and caged.

I awoke shrieking.

Had I just dreamed of Brian Bean, or had he, in fact, visited me? It was impossible to say. Regular ghost Brian Bean would have done a bit for sure. This one was so serious and foreboding. Not like him at all.

I convinced myself that it must have been a bad dream. When you are living in a nightmare and then also have a nightmare, things get a bit blurry.

Ricky the far darrig had dozed off in a folding chair

next to the levers that raise and lower the show curtains, about two short meters away from me. He had a half-eaten dinner roll balanced precariously on his furry chest while his snores shook the stacks of old props.

Nelson and Nancy were far across the theater, flirting at the merchandise table, which sells absolutely nothing anyone would want. The show cave was mostly empty, other than a few audience stragglers who were staying to try to get a dowser-graph from Equasos. (They would not. He never signs anything, as he says it "devalues" his dowser-graphs.)

The torture hose was lying uncoiled near Ricky's foot-paws, which is what far darrigs have instead of regular feet. The nozzle at the end of the hose was held loosely in his claw.

This gave me an idea—a mad idea, but it seemed possible.

With my foot, I could *just* touch the hose. I kicked off my glittery shoe and managed to get my big toe around it. I gave a little slide, and sure enough—the hose inched forward a few centimeters!

The hose ran right along the floor toward Ricky's foot-nub. I tried again and was able to nudge it a bit farther. The note from my friends was buried somewhere up in his dense red chest fur—if I could get the nozzle to slide up Ricky's body, I could maybe hook the note with the hose handle and pull it to me. It was worth a shot.

The trickiest part would be spinning the hose, ever so slightly, to get the nozzle handle in the right direction so that I might be able to rake through Ricky's fur. I tried to spin the hose with my toes when suddenly . . .

CRAMP. OW OW OW. FOOT CRAMP. OMYGOD IT HURTS SO BAD. CRAMP CRAMP CRAMP OW. CRAMPS ARE THE WORST.

My foot had seized up. Somehow my foot looked like a face that had just taken a bite out of a lemon.

When the cramp subsided, I readjusted my toes on the hose and started to nudge it again. The nozzle crept up ever so slowly and bumped against Ricky's tusk. He stirred briefly, then fell back asleep. I twisted the hose and

managed to hook the handle of the sprayer directly . . . onto Ricky's lower lip. *A serious mistake.* If I were to tug on it now, he would surely wake up.

Across the room, Nelson and Nancy looked over, but then quickly went back to giggling at the merch table, where some poor straggler was buying an overpriced *Equasos Live!* facebag.*

Nelson and Nancy were in love, and I honestly wished them the best.

I pushed the hose again and extricated the nozzle from Ricky's lip. I gave a hard wiggle to the hose, and the nozzle plopped down into the fur of his chest, not far from where I'd seen him slip the note!

I tugged at the hose as gently as possible. The nozzle started to rake through his fur, the half-eaten dinner roll

---

* Unicorns don't wear T-shirts, but they do sometimes wear facebags filled with oats, clover, or leprechaun meat.

tumbled to the ground, then POP . . . a set of keys fell out of Ricky's fur and clattered across the floor.

Ricky muttered, but did not wake up. I gave another little tug, and to my great joy, I could see the corner edge of the note hooked around the nozzle. I held my breath and tugged, gently . . . so gently. The note inched its way down his chest in the nozzle. The note popped free and fell to the floor! After a few tries I was able to drag it toward me.

Just then, Ricky fell out of his chair, crashing to the floor with a snort that scared the daylights out of me. My hand grabbed for the note and I snatched it, tucking it into my sequined leprechaun shorts. Ricky was disoriented and annoyed. He shot me a dirty look, and briefly puzzled over the placement of the hose handle so close to the Box of Death. Lucky for me, he was more interested in finding his dinner roll. He dusted it off and ate it in one bite.

He had not seen me swipe the note.

"Fifteen human minutes 'til showtime, beefie," spat Ricky at me as he wandered away, mouth full of dinner roll.

When the coast was clear, I yanked out the note and read it. Here's what it said:

Ronan, time is short, we will make this quick. We have found a way to get you out of the Cave of Miracles (hopefully) without the unicorns noticing. Be ready during your final show tonight—we will strike! Have a new clue on the whereabouts of Captain de Valera and Lily as well! Everyone sends their love.

Signed,

— Figs, Log, Rí, Cpte. Hili.

P.S. Capitaine Hili says Bon Chance and that you will know what that means!

P.P.S. EAT THIS NOTE SO THAT IT DOES NOT FALL INTO THE WRONG HANDS!!!

This was amazing news. My friends had not forsaken me. As instructed, I ate the note. This took longer than I expected. Have you ever eaten paper? If you have, it was likely by accident, like the small sticker on an apple. No biggie. This was a rather large note. As I was chewing, I wondered—why did my friends write such a short note on

such a large piece of paper? Ricky waddled back in and saw me chewing ferociously.

"Oi, did someone give you more walnuts, beefie?" he snorted as he picked up the hose and blasted me with it, and *just* as my outfit was about to be dry for the first time all day.

I choked down the paper. As horrible as it was, I had to fight a smile, as I had such joy in my heart at the idea of seeing my friends soon.

Then something bizarre happened; Equasos trotted over to me in the Box of Death. I averted my eyes as I had been instructed by Nelson, but the great unicorn himself looked directly at me! His speech was slurrier than normal. It seemed he had been celebrating the last show of the night before it even started. His breath reeked of schnapps.

"Hey beefie, I gotta tell ya—I've been at this schtick for a leprechaun lifetime and you, kid—you are the single best sidekick I've ever had," said Equasos, tapping my head with his dowser through the bars.

"R–really?" I stammered, my voice dry and raspy from

all the note eating I had recently been doing. The note was now wedged securely in the deepest part of my throat, just above my heart.

"Hooves down, the best ever," he said. "You're crushing it. Ricky was a disaster. And the thing before him—didn't even look like a leprechaun. It was some kind of goblin. Yech. Gave everybody the willies."

He made a clicking sound to Nelson, who rolled his googly eyes, then trotted over with a fresh bucket of schnapps. Equasos gulped down the bucket as he rambled on at me, nostalgic.

"When I was your age, I was the stage manager here, just like goofy eyes over there," he slurred, pointing his dowser toward Nelson. "I wanted to throw myself off the waterfall every single night. But I had something special, I had *joie de vivre*.* That's French for *chutzpah*.†

"For a while I had a real leprechaun sidekick," sloshed

---

* "Joie de vivre" is French for *joy of life*.

† "Chutzpah" is Yiddish for audacious levels of MOXIE.*

    * Moxie is slang for confidence. Sorry, I've gone down a rabbit hole here on the footnotes, and I promised myself I would not interrupt this volume. Best regards, Finbar Dowd, Deputy Commissioner.

Equasos, his dowser wobbling in the air as he pontificated. "That was an absolute muck-fest. Little pickletooter tried to kill me every show. And of course—I'm trying to 'kill' him on stage, too, but that's schtick, honey. It's all rigged. The flames, the trap doors. That real wee man—the worst. *Legit* trying to kill me. Stabbed me in the withers during the curtain call. One time he bit me right on the knee so hard I had to stop the show, and honey—you know Equasos—I don't stop this train *ever, not for nobody*, you feel me? Who bites somebody on the knee, especially during 'Everybody Get Funky,' which is my signature number?"

"*Leprechauns do!*" I thought to myself, as thinking things to myself is eighty-five percent of what Ronan Boyle does. "Leprechauns bite on the knee, during any kind of number!" But I didn't need to respond, as Equasos was on a schnapps-fueled roll. I nodded. Even if I had wanted to speak, I could not. The note was stuck in the bottom of my throat. Also, I couldn't breathe. I was choking on my own rescue note—*the irony?* I thought, with the vaguest recollection of what irony was. Tears simmered in my eyes. I gasped, but no air reached my lungs. I was dying, and

yet I could not let Equasos see that I was dying, as he would kill me.

"Anyhoo, so when I was the stage manager here, a millennia ago, my mentor, the Magnificent Fyodor—he straight-up dies on stage. And I don't mean he 'had a bad show'—I mean literally, he fell off the stage and died. LOL. Gross, right? He face-plants into the buffet of miracles. Right in the macaroni, and then he drowned. *Drowned in macaroni.* Can you imagine? Yech. I mean, the macaroni here is to die for, but not like that, honey!"

And then I died.

No kidding, according to Nelson the stage manager I was legally dead for the better part of two minutes. Then he revived me with several good hoof kicks to the midsection and a bucket of room-temperature schnapps in my face.

I'm sure you are wondering: *"Ronan Boyle, what happens when you die?"* Well, I can't say that this is the case for everybody, but for me, when I died, I saw a very bright light. I thought about that time that I tried to high-five Yogi Hansra.

Then a figure came to me from the light. He took my arm and we sat back onto a comfortable four-person ski lift.

"Hello, Ronan. I'm Pierce Brosnan," said Pierce Brosnan, the handsome actor of fame, originally of County Louth, Ireland, later of the world stage and screen. The ski lift zipped us up through the clouds on a perfect winter day.

"You're here for Dame Judi's mixer, of course," continued Pierce Brosnan, making a few notes on a clipboard he carried and affixing a green wristband around my wrist.

"I am?" I asked, unaware that I was dead, and this was the next dimension I had entered.

"Indeed you are, so young, and yet—we're glad to have you, Ronan Janet. Don't lose that wristband, as you will need it for the room full of complimentary berets."

"But," I protested, "I don't understand why I'm here with you, specifically, Mr. Brosnan?"

"Ah, of course. You forget my relationship to Dame Judi," explained Pierce Brosnan in the loveliest accent you've ever heard. "I was James Bond when Dame Judi reinvented the role of 'M' and the Bond movies still had a sense of fun to them. Before we all started to take ourselves too seriously."

"Of course!" I cheered in this other dimension, literally smacking my own face. "This makes perfect sense. Wonderful. What a treat! I'm so glad to meet you," I rambled on, shaking his hand with too much enthusiasm.

"It will all become clear to you soon, Ronan Janet," said Pierce Brosnan. "You've left your human body behind, and you're headed to a mixer that Dame Judi is throwing in a very bright cloud in what you would think of as space, but what angels know as the former planet of Pluto. But please don't worry, it's a very casual affair. Just some pass-arounds, pressed sandwiches, and of course the beret gifting room."

My mouth hung slack. Moments ago I was dying in a cage in Bad Aonbheannach. Now I was being escorted to a casual mixer with one of the very solid James Bonds. I could already feel that my various allergies had vanished. My nostrils were wide open. Not even one part of my body was itchy (and this is rare in our dimension).

"I think you're going to like it here, Ronan Janet," said

Pierce Brosnan, giving me a little wink. "And a great friend of yours is already with us."

"*Hello, I'm David Beckham, welcome to McDonald's, can I take your order?*"

The ghost of Brian Bean had materialized next to Pierce Brosnan. I was delighted to see him. He was doing the bit I had suggested to him in a dream: *David Beckham working the drive-through.* It wasn't a perfect bit, and honestly, I've heard a lot of David Beckham impressions in my life, so it felt a bit tired. Still, I laughed hard, feeling happier than I had ever felt before.

And then a unicorn hoof kicked me in the midsection so hard that I barfed up a walnut. Ugh.

I was back in Tir Na Nog.

"Is he dead?" asked Equasos with zero panic in his voice.

"Not quite, sir," replied Nelson, with that pleasant whistle between his teeth.

"Good. He's the best sidekick I ever had. I love this li'l beefie. Wake up, kid—you're about to get a raise. That is, if you're not dead."

I blinked and wheezed for a moment, fumbling around

for my glasses. My throat was burning from the choking, and my sternum was bruised from Nelson's hoof kick. But somehow, in all of this something ever so strange was happening. It was a feeling I wasn't quite accustomed to.

I was happy. Genuinely happy. Because I knew what was waiting for me in the next dimension: some kind of mixer with my favorite actress and pressed sandwiches. But deep down, I was mostly proud that I was doing a good job for Equasos here in the Cave of Miracles. Maybe playing a hapless leprechaun sidekick nine times a day for retired unicorns was my destiny. Perhaps Captain de Valera and Lily had already escaped the weegees and were fine?

I could just *stay here.* Back in the human Republic of Ireland, my parents were museum types, and they were never overeager to praise me willy-nilly. Captain Fearnley, my mentor in the Galway Garda, said many kind things to me, *I think*—but I cannot be sure, as I could never understand his country accent. This praise from Equasos, a drunken lavender unicorn with a weight problem and major rage issues, was *the most positive feedback I'd ever gotten in my life.*

Was this a horrible job? Technically, yes. Was I locked

in a cage between shows and paid in damp walnuts? Yes—but even Equasos knew that *I was nailing it.* For perhaps the first time in my life, I felt like I deserved to be where I was. The teensiest, tiniest part of me felt bad that I was plotting my escape this very night, during the show that was about to begin. I was about to betray Equasos and I knew he would not take it well. He doesn't even take *good news* well.

"Anyhoo, make sure this kid gets some extra walnuts," whinnied Equasos at Ricky as he trotted toward the stage, his hooves looping and tripping over one another in his soggy state. Ricky threw a few damp walnuts at me—hard.

"Ooooooh. Everybody loves the new beefie, isn't he wonderful? Puts Ricky to shame, doesn't he!? *Blah blah hooray for the beefie,*" sneered Ricky as his paw-foot gave me a swift kick to the bottom. "And don't you forget—it's five hundred euros if you want that note from your beautiful pig friend!"

Ricky reached into his fur for the note, but of course he couldn't find it, as it was in my stomach! His eyes darted around the room angrily. He patted himself down. Then patted me up and down, but of course—found nothing. Then he let out a very sad howl, which is the kind of noise far darrigs make, inflating the little pouch under his tusks like a balloon—it was so loud that it would cause a ringing in my ears that would last for several days. Ricky gave me an extra hard blast with the hose, then threw one last walnut right at my nose.

I could hear the first notes of "Hoofin' It off to Where We Can Kill a Leprechaun for Free." The show was about to start. Hopefully, I would be out of this stunning cave and buffet within the hour. But either way, I knew one thing for sure . . .

. . . that I would give the performance of a lifetime.

Chapter Eight
THE WATERCOMBS

While I had vowed to give the performance of my life, Equasos was very off in this last show of the night. When he sang "Mister, Don't You Poop on My Haypile, Please" (a pretty simple soft-hoof number) he messed up the words so badly that they came out as: "Sister Juan's Tooth Is in Apoplexy"—lyrics that make even less sense than the real ones, which are nonsense to begin with.

I scanned the lackluster crowd for any sign of Log, Capitaine Hili, Figs, or Rí the wolfhound—but there was no trace, and they certainly would have stood out, as the audience was barely half full, which always makes the buffet seem to stretch even longer.

Sadly for Equasos, I could clearly spot a newspaper critic, sitting right up front, making notes in a pad with her dowser. She looked mortified.

The rest of the crowd didn't seem to mind that Equasos was phoning it in. These were older unicorns, with glassy eyes, puffing on pipes, or devouring huge piles of macaroni from the buffet. They would mouth along with the words to every song, except for "(Everybody) Get Funky," which must have been from an era when Equasos was trying to reinvent himself. It didn't jibe with the rest of his catalog. You could feel the oxygen get sucked out of the room when "(Everybody) Get Funky" began. It was also the number when the buffet line was always the longest.

Yet I, Ronan Janet Boyle, was crushing this show.

My yelps and screams were as close to the real screaming a leprechaun would do as you could imagine. In my mind I started musking, which is when frightened leprechauns make a foul smell. Perhaps it was just the crunchy,

horrible outfit and two days of boat travel—but I felt like I was giving off a real musk. *I was in the moment.* The retired unicorns in the crowd sincerely looked like they wanted to kill me (a compliment, of course).

During the bridge of "Poke, Poke, Poke dat Wee Man, Poke dat Wee Man Good," when Equasos stabs me with his dowser and I fall down "dead" through the trap door— what was waiting for me below the stage made me gasp.

I was told to be ready for anything, but of course I wasn't, as being unprepared is almost a part of my personality.

In the crawlspace below the stage, Log MacDougal was squatting, shillelagh at the ready, Rí the wolfhound at her side. Combined, they were certainly the largest animals that had ever been crammed into this crawlspace. Log had Ricky the far darrig trapped in her arm, her tattooed hand over his mouth. He struggled, but as Log is ten times stronger than any human I'd ever met, a cynical far darrig was no match for her.

"Hehehehehe, hello Ronan," giggled Log, "up for a little excursion?"

I couldn't help but give Log a massive hug. This was a bit

awkward, as Ricky the far darrig was a hostage in her arm, and unwittingly became the third participant in this hug. He was annoyed, even by his standards.

"Now little far darrig," whispered Log, "me, my mate, and this bloodthirsty hound are going to walk right out of here, and if you follow us, I'll snap your tusks right off and poke 'em in your eyes—I've done it before."

This was absolute blarney (not true). Log had never hurt a far darrig, nor would she. And Rí was an excellent dad of one of the younger wolfhounds in the Special Unit named Pedro. But Log was playing the part of a thug beautifully.

"Wait, my uniform. My shillelagh, my shenanogram," I whispered. "I can't leave here in sequin shorts! I'm on two vendetti!"*

"It's quite fetching on you," giggled Log as she turned to Ricky. "Bring us his uniform, or I'll snap your tusks off." Log gave Ricky a squeeze that made his eyes bulge and caused him to let out a sad little toot from his bottom.

---

* Not a word.

"Easy, easy! I'm the beefie's friend—haven't I been a friend to you, beefie?" said Ricky to me, his eyes pleading. "I gave you such fine walnuts, and kept you nice and fresh with the gentle hose."

I shot Ricky a dirty look. We both knew this was a revisionist notion of our relationship. *Gentle hose?* Trust me, it was set on "jet" or whatever unicorns call that setting.

"Get his clothes and shillelagh, now," whispered Log.

"And the beret—so important! It doesn't work without the beret," I added, because, as you know, I love the optional Special Unit beret.

"One funny move and . . ." Log made a gesture that suggested tusks getting snapped in half.

Log loosened her grip. Ricky rubbed his throat with his paw, wounded and embarrassed. He scurried away into the shadows. Above us, I could hear Equasos's hooves missing their marks. He and Nancy were getting to "Get Out of My Dreams and into This Harness," which was bad news for me—as it's immediately before the curtain call when I

was expected to pop up through a trap door so that Equasos could set me on fire.

It felt like a lifetime passed. Ricky was taking forever. Maybe he wasn't coming back at all? I did not look forward to fleeing Bad Aonbheannach in this sequin outfit that crept up my bottom cheeks. Shockingly, a moment later, Ricky scampered back and passed me a garment bag and my shillelagh.

"Good luck then, beefie," said Ricky, with a glint in his eye. "I wish you well. I'll need that outfit back, as I suppose I'll have to play the wee man again."

I could see that Ricky was *thrilled* to be getting rid of me, as it meant he would be recast in his old role of Leprechaun Number One. There was an ever-so-tiny smile around his tusks, and I understood. There is a joy to being on the legitimate stage that is difficult to describe—a rush of adrenaline that is addictive.

For no obvious reason, I gave Ricky a hug. He pretended to be cross with me, but his body language was warm. He patted my shoulder with his paw.

"Take care in the watercombs, beefie," said Ricky, "nasty things in there."

"Careful in the . . . what now?" I handed Ricky the sequin outfit as I fumbled into my kilt and beret.

Rí nudged me toward a vent below the stage. A metal grate had been punched in by Log MacDougal, as it would have taken someone as strong as her to do this. Punching things is Log's superpower.

Log and Rí had found their way to me through the watercombs of Bad Aonbheannach—the complex waterworks of tubes and tunnels that runs behind the cliff wall of the city and under the many spa baths. The flow of the watercombs also powers the locks and dams that bring boats up and down over Arthur falls, as well as a hydroelectric generator that lights up the many showrooms and karaoke lounges of the city. Tragically for those using it to escape, it also happens to be part of the city's sanitation system. Yes, some of the tubes in the watercombs are used to flush unicorn poop out of the city. A city with a lot

of unicorns in the high season. I wish I could tell you that we did not have to pass through one or two of these terrible poopways on our escape, but that would be untrue.

Here are a few things you would find in the water-combs of Bad Aonbheannach, in order from least scary, to most scary:

1. Skeletons of unicorns, stacked neatly for the past few thousand years, which gives the water tunnels the catacombs part of their name.
2. Rats the size of teenage wolfhounds.
3. Literal rivers of unicorn poop.
4. The complete absence of even the tiniest sliver of daylight.

Rí led the way. A dog's nose is the only reliable guide in the pitch black. Keep in mind, Rí had to find his way *out* of this massive labyrinth of tubes the same way he had found me, only by smell. And to do that, he would have to block out the aroma of unicorn poop, which is a trick. I held on to his tail. Log shuffled along behind me, sometimes her huge shoulders rubbing each side of the tubes.

I did not anticipate what would happen when I encountered the first of the mega-rats. You know the old maxim people love to say about how animals are "more scared of you than you are of them"? Well, this is very true of the large rats in the watercombs. They are the most scaredy-cat creatures I have ever encountered. I can't say that I've *seen* them per se, as it's pitch black in the tubes, but every one that bumped into me screamed like bloody murder and panicked. You could hear the rats yelling to each other, things like: "Oh my God! There's something in the tubes!" and "EWWWWW HOLY MUCK, I JUST BRUSHED INTO SOMETHING." (Log kindly translated the screams for me, as they were in the language of the animals.)

The next three hours were like a horror movie from the reverse point of view, in which me and my mates were the monsters, and the plump rats were the heroes, running away from us.

If I never hear a gaggle of super-rats screaming again, it'll be too soon. At a few points I tried my best to have Log tell them: "Hello! Just two humans and a friendly wolf-hound here, nothing to be frightened of!" But it was to no avail. The rats seemed to be very dimwitted. They did lots of things that unwise humans do in horror movies. They would *back up* into us and scream, they would *split up*, then run into us and *scream*. None of them had a plan other than to run and scream.

I genuinely wondered what they thought we would do to them? *Eat them?* Ugh. Plump rats that have been marinating in unicorn poop for their entire lives? No, thank you very much! I don't even eat shrimp or popcorn. God forbid pop-corn shrimp.

Rí was doing his best to navigate. His nose was pumping air like a well-made Dustbuster. We arrived at what felt to be a metal hatch. I could hear water was dripping around the seal. We'd been steadily climbing in the tubes for a human hour.

"Well done, Rí," Log said. "This hatch should put us

under the top part of the falls. It opens *underneath* the river. So once through the hatch, hold your breath as long as you can. I'll try to pull it closed after us." Then Log repeated this to Rí in the language of the animals.

We all held our breath. Log spun the valve on the hatch and a zillion gallons of water rushed down on us.

I would not have made it through, had Rí not pulled me up by the shillelagh hooks on the back of my jacket. I remember thinking that I was about to drown and that wolfhounds were surprisingly good swimmers. Log squeezed through behind us and somehow managed to seal the hatch behind her—this was quite a feat, as she was fighting the full power flow of the River of GLOOM.

My lungs were on fire. Rí's teeth had lost their grip on me. I was disoriented, swimming in the direction I suspected was up, but this was more of a feeling than a fact. As I was about to run out of air, my beret bonked against something big and metal. I pulled myself along until I finally came to the surface of the river, panting, barely alive.

The last few moments were pure terror, but it did get the last traces of unicorn poop out of my kilt.

Capitaine Hili looked down at me from the deck of the *ucky evil*. Clearly she did not recognize me. At some point in my captivity she must have turned invisible and reset her memory* to back to blank. It would take much of the rest of the evening to catch her up on things.

"*Enchantee! Je suis Capitaine Hili, petit* leprechaun. *Très* handsome, zis one!"

In all the chaos, I had forgotten that I still had a long red beard glued to my face.

---

* Some consider the Tokoloshe trait of forgetting their entire life each time they turn invisible as a negative—BUT there are also well-regarded articles in Faerie and Human Science Journals that prove that the Tokoloshe quite *love* this phenomenon, and wouldn't change it even if they could. Imagine being able to hear your favorite joke thousands of times, as if for the first time. Every Tokoloshe kiss is a first kiss, the kind that makes your heart race.

Rí popped up beside me, paddling like a crazed Chihuahua. Log surfaced a moment later and pulled me toward the ladder of the *ucky evil*, which took me back to the moment that she had saved my life on Frolic Day during our training in Killarney.

"You're a sight for sore eyes, Ronan Boyle! We thought we'd lost you to the sharpies!" said Figs, using a derogatory word for unicorns as we flopped onto the main deck. "And I love the beard. Can't believe you grew a long red beard in a day. Humans—they never cease to amaze!"

"Figs!" I rasped. "I can't tell you how good it is to see you! I've been living on walnuts and the finest water I've ever tasted. Also I was in a show, and—going by crowd reaction—I think I was pretty great in it."

"Well, you're safe now," said Figs, totally ignoring my triumph in the unicorn theater. "And I truly hate to do this, but you may have been compromised by the unicorns, so—you're under arrest."

And then my friend Horatio Fitzmartin Dromgool, a naked little man with a hat, clapped handcuffs around my wrists.

Chapter Nine
A CLUE

For the next little bit I was a prisoner in the hold of the *ucky evil*, in a metal box that was once used to hold some manner of small livestock. The irony that this box was identical to the Box of Death that Equasos had kept me in was not lost on me. Only now I was being held by my own pretty-good friends.

"It's a technicality, Ronan. It's the protocol!" protested Figs as he passed me a warm pressed truffle and gouda sandwich through the bars.*

---

* All Special Unit operatives carry a sandwich press to make the Irish Goodbye, a sandwich that can wipe the memory of lookie-loos to traumatic incidents with the faerie folk, but—it can also be used for personal

"Let me out! This is demeaning and annoying," I protested. "This is no way to treat a Detective of the Special Unit! I have a valid BeefCard! And holy cow this sandwich is amazing, thank you very much, Figs!"

"Orders is orders. When I reported you kidnapped by the unicorns, I got a sheerie from Commander McManus with precise instructions. With your parents' prison break, and their ties to known associates of the weegees and all that, I can't let you out until I verify that you have not been compromised by the unicorns. The CAPTCHA test must be performed!†

(*cont.*) sandwiches, as long as they don't have classified ingredients. This is why almost all officers of the Special Unity put on the "Noobster-Fifteen" in their first year on the job, as eating pressed sandwhiches slathered with cheese and rich Irish butter is a great way to keep weight *on*.

† CAPTCHA is an acronym for Catching Any Possible Tricksters who Can't Humanize ASAP. It's designed to filter out wee folk. Yes, the acronym for CAPTCHA includes *another* acronym: ASAP, which stands for As Soon As Possible. I was not on the committee that invented or named this. It's the brainchild of Finbar Dowd, Deputy Commissioner of the Special Unit, who is as drab as a potato, and whose face I could not remember if you gave me a million euros.

"And Ronan, this big beard of yours isn't helping your case," added Figs, troubled. "It's exactly the kind of whiskers a leprechaun would have."

"Because it's a fake beard that has been glued to my face!" I protested. "LET ME OUT! I NEED TO SEE THIS CLUE YOU'VE FOUND!"

The wee folk are tricksters who love to swap human babies and even human senior citizens for logs. Sadly, it's not uncommon for Special Unit officers to become compromised when they spend too much time in the company of the wee folk.

On occasion, a Special Unit officer will return from Tir Na Nog as what's called a *sleeper*, doing the dirty work of the filthy leprechauns. There was a case during my training at Collins House when a Special Unit Detective returned from a years-long undercover operation in Glenavy. She tried to convince her human colleagues at Collins House that they should invest in a set of magic fiddles she was selling whose music was so bittersweet, it made those who heard it weep tears of delicious beer. So she made money

on the fiddles *and* the beer. And there were LOTS of fiddles to buy in the package. The whole thing was a classic leprechaun pyramid scheme. The officer had been so long undercover with the leprechauns in Glenavy that she was actually made in the leprechaun mafia as *foaibas*, which is what they call an *underboss*.

Some aspects of the CAPTCHA test are classified, but it involves the officer who is administering the test to open a box of small items that the wee folk could not possibly refuse: treasure map, invisible Ed Sheehan tickets, unicorn bones, shoe buckles of Queen Moira with the Magnificent Forehead, and a copy of William Butler Yeats's famous poem "When You Are Old."

To you and I this list may sound silly. (Sure, I *like* Yeats's famous poem, and it makes me a bit sad. But leprechauns find it to be HILARIOUS. They can't get enough of it. I don't quite get what's so funny about it. Perhaps it's because leprechauns don't really grow old, so to them this poem is just a goof.)

If you were to hold up a pair of "invisible Ed Sheeran

tickets" to a leprechaun—they would rip them out of your hands and bolt through the wall, leaving a leprechaun-shaped hole. They wouldn't even think to check if the tickets were legitimate until they showed up at the venue.

Most humans, of course, will bristle at the notion of being offered invisible things, which is why the CAPTCHA test generally has an accuracy rate of ninety-nine percent.

I passed the CAPTCHA test with ease. Figs embraced me, which was uncomfortable, as he was back to being a little naked hedgehog covered in spikes. There was the faint trace of hot pickle on his breath, and I was reasonably sure he'd been giving himself picklefits below deck when nobody was around. I know I had heard some ceiling bonks from between the irresistible nineties hip-hop rhythm of the *ucky evil*'s steam engine.

I was starving. I scarfed down both the second and third pressed sandwiches that Figs made for me. If you haven't had a pressed sandwich, you truly haven't lived. Pressed sandwiches are the Dame Judi Dench of the sandwich catalog.

We climbed up to the main deck of the *ucky evil*, where Rí was leaning out over the bow of the ship, like a living masthead, sniffing the river for trouble (which was coming quite soon).

Log was sitting on the starboard side, her feet dangling off the boat. Log's tree-trunk legs are so long that her toes would occasionally dip in and out of the warm bubbling river. She was giggling to herself and carving a new tattoo on her already-crowded arm with a sharp little pin. It was crude, but I could tell it was me in my sequin leprechaun shorts outfit, my eyes wide in panic, my bottom on fire.

"Whaddaya think, boyo?" giggled Log.

"Very nice, I hope it hurts for a long time," I said, totally kidding because I love Log.

Capitaine Hili approached me, wobbling a little bit on her tentacle feet. She had changed into a T-shirt that read: MY KIDS WENT TO THE STRANGE PLACE IN THE BOGLANDS AND ALL I GOT WAS THIS LOUSY T-SHIRT. It was becoming clear to me that Capitaine Hili has one of my very least favorite

character traits: being a wearer of funny T-shirts. I have no idea where I get this aversion, possibly from some childhood trauma. In spite of the T-shirts, I was quite fond of the capitaine. And, of course, I coveted her magnificent rungu.

"Roxanne Boyle," she said, getting my name very wrong but in a fun way. "You need zee vinegar! Toot de suite." She grabbed a filthy bottle and poured me a tall glass. The smell was horrendous.

"Um, no thank you. No vinegar for me," I replied.

"Non. Is not for drink. Vinegar eesss magic, *ca va*?" She winked at me.

This last sentence I did not understand.

"Zee vinegar, make clean anyzing!" she said as she poured some vinegar into a rag and began to rub it on my cheeks.

It hurt a bit, and stung my eyes, but a few seconds later, with a satisfying RRRRIIIIP, I was beard free. The vinegar burned right through the spirit gum and the beard came right

off. My cheeks were free! I felt alive again. My face, which is often pink, bloomed into the color of an amaranth, which is a very red plant. As it turns out, vinegar cleans lots of things. I would learn more than I ever wanted to know about this subject in a book that Capitaine Hili handed me called *How to Clean Anything with Vinegar* by Capitaine Jaqueline Hili. Then there was a strange moment where it became clear I was supposed to *purchase* this book from Capitaine Hili.

There is nothing in the world more uncomfortable than when a friend writes a book, and you are expected to buy it. Ugh. And then they ask if you want it signed, but of course, YOU DON'T, because you can't regift a book that has been signed to you.

The *ucky evil* was at anchor, at a bend where the River of GLOOM divides into three tributaries: one that leads Downnog into the Lower Unknown, one that flows Upnog and connects to the Stream of Whiskey and is the main route to the Strange Place in the Boglands, and one toward ? (which is an actual direction on leprechaun maps) Coast and the city of North Ifreann.

Which route the weegees had taken with the captain

and Lily was anybody's guess. Hopefully the clue that Figs had found would help sort it out.

Figs had púca-shifted into a stag, which is the most striking of his animal forms I had yet seen. His hat perched precariously on his impressive rack of antlers. Stag-form Figs is almost imposing (at least compared to his pig and hedgehog forms).

"My cousin Danny is a púca who works as a bouncer in one of the '80s discotheques of Bad Aonbheannach. Danny knows everybody. When your friends passed through town with the weegees, a note fell into his hands, through a haretroll that owes him a favor," said Figs.

"Another note! Excellent!" The riddle from the captain had been a piece of cake for me. (When it's not regretting my every move or talking to Dame Judi, my brain loves riddles and puzzles.) "Let's see it!"

A hangdog look came across Figs's face.

"Well . . . that's just it. There's a bit of a glitch, Ronan," said stag-form Figs.

"A glitch. What kind of glitch?"

Figs and Hili exchanged a nervous look.

"A major glitch. I'm afraid that the haretroll got the note to Danny just as he was about to shift into his goat form. You know we púcas can't control our shape-shifting. We have no say in the matter. It's not his fault, really."

"Yes, of course," I replied, started to get very concerned. "Just let me see it!"

"I'm afraid that Danny . . . how can I put this? Danny accidentally chewed up the note from your friends," said Figs.

"Chewed up?"

Figs tipped his antlers and dumped out the remnants of what was once a note—now just random letters in the handwriting of Captain Siobhán de Valera. Tragically faded by a bit of goat spit. It was a disaster. I put all the pieces of the note faceup on the deck. The loose letters spelled out:

ATAEMNIHTSECFOPDAWR

Nothing. This is not a word. Not even in Irish. Yes, I checked. Not even the name of an Irish town.*

---

* This was not totally improbable, as Ballaghnatrillick and Cloontyprocklis are actual towns in Ireland.

I would have to rearrange the letters until I found something that made sense. Luckily, other than shrimp allergies, finding lost words is as close to a superpower as I have.

I began sliding the letters around. Here's what I came up with (maddeningly almost always with stray letters left over!):

Imps! Can dean warn of pen?

Rain paris, don't we coup?

Trains eat of wasp mathcad!

I ate the fast soup, man

Drama of eatin' maps!

Fear of dis tin man

Pa's camp is raw, mad

Woman in the toast puf'd

O sir, dan wears tan chimp

I cope when is forced, Marc

Cup from the war of dance

His name is "power damp"

Prams r of wee nate's doin'

And of course: cod fart menu

I would repeat this process for almost a human hour with no outcome that made any sense at all. Even worse, COD FART MENU kept coming up, because sometimes once you see a word pattern, it becomes impossible to unsee it.

Log tried a few in the language of the faerie folk, and the language of the animals, just in case. Capitaine Hili came up with a few in French that were equally nonsensical.

It felt like time to give up. Hope was lost. This mission was a failure. So much time squandered in the Steps, in Bad Aonbheannach. Why had the commissioner allowed me to take this mission when I was so unqualified? Dermot Lally would have already found them with his one eye! *You're only in the Special Unit because Captain de Valera needed to use you as a pole in a small hole in Clifden Castle, Ronan! That's why. You're a fraud.* Dame Judi was pacing in the wings, about to make her entrance in my mind, dressed as Titania from *Midsummer Night's Dream*—a character that she's played twice—FORTY-TWO YEARS APART! *Wow.*

I should be in school like a normal boy. Even that eejit Finbar Dowd could have handled this better.*

I took off my glasses. My underachieving eyes were exhausted. I couldn't even see words anymore. Just an infuriating jumble of goat-spit-soaked letters. And every minute squandered, with the captain's and Lily's fate in the hands of the horrible weegees!

---

* *Hello. Finbar Dowd here in the footnotes. I don't mean to interrupt Ronan Boyle's existential crisis, as these are very legitimate questions. Not the part about me being an eejit. I'm runner-up employee of the month several times at Collins House! Apparently there's a name for Ronan's condition known as Imposter Syndrome, where one feels that their achievements are based on luck. Anyway: I really just wanted to point out that Ronan Boyle, being fifteen and indeed underqualified for this mission, has missed MAJOR SYMBOLISM in his Dame Judi daydream! It struck me plain as day: DID YOU SEE IT? IT'S SO OBVIOUS!*

Dame Judi = Ronan's alter ego. Respected authority figure, seemingly without self-doubt. Dressed as TITANIA!!! Titania = LITERALLY the "Queen of the Faeries" in Shakespeare's delightful three-and-a-half-hour-long comedy A Midsummer Night's Dream! Does this not represent Captain de Valera, authority figure of the Faerie Police!? All of his mental health problems are converging into a PERFECT STORM! Poor Lieutenant Boyle! And he didn't even notice!

Yes! Finbar Dowd, armchair psychiatrist! Amateur Theatrical, collector of humorous salt and pepper shakers, at your service! Now then, I will NOT under any circumstances interrupt these journals again. And a reminder that if Lieutenant Boyle's belt is returned complete, the reward comes with a coupon to the wonderful Collins House Cafeteria. Best, F.D.

And then I saw it.

Only with my blurry eyes was it possible. How I hadn't seen it before I don't know. I gasped. If I told you that tears did not well up in my eyes, it would be a lie. When assembled correctly, the captain's note was plain as day, even the cursive letters connecting to each other at the shredded edges. The letters read:

SWAMP OF CERTAIN DEATH

I let out a trademark shriek. The Swamp of Certain Death lies just between us and North Ifreann. Everyone sprang into action. Log spun me in the air. The capitaine called out to the wheelhouse.

"Set a course for zee Swamp of Certain Death. Toot de suite!"

I wasn't sure to whom Capitaine Hili was yelling. Later I learned that the *ucky evil* has an autopilot system that involves an enchanted old mop tied to the steering wheel. (Not coincidentally, this autopilot system was put into place for those many occasions when the capitaine cannot

remember that she is a boat captain. There's a decent argument that the enchanted mop is a *slightly* better captain than Hili herself.)

The engine of the *ucky evil* belched, and we veered hard to starboard, chugging into the smallest, darkest, and most frightening and overgrown of the three tributaries.

I wiped my happy tears and curled up next to Rí in the bow of the ship. We watched as the dark vegetation of the shoreline began to envelop the river. The River of GLOOM was becoming a swamp. I could hear the hull as it scraped on the glowing branches that rose up around us from the murk.

My heart was racing. We were back on the scent! I pulled out my notebook and hastily wrote three letters.

The first letter was to my parents, Brendan and Fiona Boyle, whom I missed terribly, and for whom I was genuinely concerned. I knew they had joined the famous gangs in Mountjoy Prison mostly for the social aspect and camaraderie. But now they had escaped, out on the mean streets of Dublin or who-knows-where with these frightening gang people. Mum and Da are museum types. My mum has a PhD in Irish history. A terrible thought that went through my head: *What if my parents, falsely imprisoned for a crime that was in truth committed by Lord Desmond Dooley, had become* actual *criminals from spending time in prison?!* This sort of thing happens! I'm sure there is a name for this phenomenon and that there are documentaries about it.

Here's the letter I wrote to Mum and Da. (In verse, which becomes a bit of a habit after Special Unit training.)

Mum and Da,
I'm heading up the River of GLOOM,
and I know this won't get to you anytime soon
But I've heard you escaped from your cells in Mountjoy,
And this news has the power to truly annoy—
Your son, Ronan Janet. I'm sick to my stomach!
I'm pinker than normal, entirely flummoxed.
I feel that your judgment is reckless and errant,
like our places are swapped, as if I were your parents.
It's so disconcerting, I'm going insane
while I'm on some vendetti to clear both your names!
All that I am asking, whatever you do:

Is steer clear of crimes, and please NO TATTOOS.
I'll bring back the Bog Man, whatever it takes,
please turn yourselves in, don't compound your mistakes.
You know that I love you both beyond words,
If I had to describe it, it would sound absurd.
You are the best parents, on this whole blue planet
Regards, your Detective (and son) Ronan Janet

The next letter was to my hilarious and unreliable guardian Dolores Mullen, back in Galway. I missed her terribly.

You wonderful tart,
I hope you exist.
Of the people I miss,
You're top three on the list.
I hope that your fiddle is cheering the folk,
on Shop Street in Galway or Buttermilk Walk.
I miss your round face, and sometimes I wonder,
is your hair still pink, or some new bizarre color?
I'm on a vendetta, and so far so good,
I'd mail you this letter if only I could.
Until we meet next, which I hope is quite soon,
take care of yourself, you magnificent loon.

The last letter I wrote was to Captain de Valera, prisoner of the weegees and the Bog Man. I finished it and then I tore it up immediately, for both classified and personal reasons, because perhaps I had overstepped.

My feelings for Captain de Valera are purely admiration.

I'm certain of this fact. The same way you would only love your teacher when you are in elementary school and then accidentally call her Mum and feel like an eejit and now I'm going on too long on this subject and probably a lot of it has to do with her cool uniform and the boots and the hair and the mismatched eyes and such.

Of course, there was no way to mail these letters, unless I found a stray sheerie* who could courier to the human realm for me, and there was none around.

---

* A sheerie is the ghost of a faerie. They can transport humans and small items great distances in a short time. These travel requests can only be approved by the rank of captain or above, and they usually only work within ONE travel zone. Early efforts to travel Special Unit officers between Tir Na Nog and the human Republic of Ireland (Zones 1 and 2) resulted in the officers turning into a thick gelatinous goo that smelled like cheeseburger soup—which is a real thing.

The truth is, I was only acting brave on these vendetti for Log's and Rí's sake, but deep down in my stomach I knew that perhaps I had been called up to the Special Unit too young. I was only fifteen years old, the youngest cadet ever in the Special Unit. I was never the boldest person before all of this. When I was an intern in the Galway Garda, I kept the batteries separate from my torch, so as not to accidentally turn on the light when it was in my holster. I was acting brave right now because I wanted to see Lily again.

And I wanted to see the captain, whom I am not in love with. Besides, she was probably something like six years older than me.

I fell asleep on top of Rí, a warm breeze wafting over us, lovely dog smell filling my nose. I dreamed that I was back in Wolfdew with Lily, reading a book on a rainy Saturday afternoon, watching her drift in and out of sleep in the wonderful way only a dog can do.

When I awoke sometime later, I distinctly thought I heard the sound of Figs pickletooting and bumping into the ceiling below deck. I made a note to talk to him about the dangers of wasting your life chasing the picklefits.

Up ahead I could see thatch rooftops rising out of the water, as if a leprechaun village had been flooded to nearly the tops of the houses. Hedgehog-form Figs came above deck and explained that this underwater town was called Freetown, built by a group of expat merrows who live below the surface, having fled the persecution and biting of sharks in the Irish Sea. Merrows tend to give me a case of the willies, so I wasn't hoping to run into any, and fortunately we did not, just a few bubbles on the surface indicating that they must be moving around below us.

The air was getting sultry. I am not a fan of the word *sultry*, but I can't think of any other word to describe the wet dense air that clung like papier-mâché to the face and clothing. It was so, well—sultry. Bad kilt weather.

The *ucky evil* had sputtered to a crawl to navigate the swamp. This area of the river Downnog of the Swamp of Certain Death has the accurate name Confusing Huge-fruits. The trees in this area bear the largest fruits you have ever seen. Huge fruits, but in confusing colors that don't make sense to the human eye. We passed a pear tree where each fruit was taller than Log MacDougal and the colors of a tiger. An orange tree where each fruit would take ten strong humans to roll it, and for some reason the oranges had bright blue feathers instead of orange rind. It was so, so confusing.

"Regarde! Regarde!" shouted Hili from the wheelhouse. She was pointing toward a leopard-print banana that was drifting straight at us. This was disconcerting, as the banana was a good deal longer than the *ucky evil*, which is a decent-sized houseboat.

Either Capitaine Hili or (more likely) the mop diverted the boat around it. The engine's sputtering slowed as the hugefruit trees rose up all around us, their roots rising out of the water, creating little caverns below them.

Hedgehog–form Figs approached me, nervous, his eyes scanning out into the swamp. The sun was beginning to set.

"Oh dear. I was truly hoping ol' moppy could get us to the Swamp of Certain Death before nightfall. Between us, the enchanted mop does *most* of the driving of the ship. Capitaine Hili is a nice lady, but purely a figurehead." Figs's spikes bristled a bit as he muttered, "Come on, moppy. I'd love to be out of the swamp before nightfall. I didn't want to be here after nightfall."

"Why? What happens at nightfall?" I asked.

Chapter Ten
NIGHTFALL

The second half of the fifth century was a humdinger for Ireland. A young British boy was brought to the Emerald Isle by Irish pirates. You thought regular pirates didn't care about dental hygiene? Wait 'til you meet Irish pirates! Yikes. The worst. The songs that Irish pirates sing have lyrics so filthy that you will spend a year in prison in any civilized European country just for humming along with them.

The boy was an enslaved worker for six years, doing chores for pirates who were as lazy as they were filthy. Then, in what must have been an action sequence worthy of a film starring a dirt-covered Colin Farrell in a tunic, the boy karate chopped, punched, and kicked his way to freedom, busting noses, swinging on ropes, and snapping the arms of Irish pirates.

In my mind's eye, portions of this boy's escape are in slow motion set to the song "Mama Said Knock You Out."

The boy went to France, studied to be a cleric, and returned to Ireland as a missionary. Maybe you're thinking this young boy would go on to be known as Pirate Fighter, but no, even better—he would go on to be known as Saint Patrick, the patron saint of Ireland.

When Saint Patrick returned to the Emerald Isle, he did two things: He tried to make everybody follow the new religion that he was working for, and he banished all of the snakes. Yes, there is not one single snake on the island of Ireland. Why? Because of Saint Patrick. Where on Earth did he send all those snakes?

The answer is that they were banished to Tir Na Nog, very specifically to the Swamp of Certain Death. The very same swamp we were currently chugging through at one nautical kilometer per hour, in a rusted houseboat, piloted by a mop and her charming Tokoloshe sidekick.

When the sun goes down, the snakes come out.

All. Of. Them.

The snakes have been living here (and multiplying) for almost sixteen hundred years with no natural predators. The snakes haven't just survived, they have thrived. Little snakes? *Check.* Poisonous snakes? *You bet.* Anacondas? *Sure thing, pal!*

At dusk, the surface of the Swamp of Certain Death becomes—not figuratively—a*ll snakes.* It's a rush hour of snakes, going—well—wherever snakes go.

It's not that they are evil snakes, per se. Nor can they talk. The snakes have no real agenda. They have regular snake attributes. The frightening part is the *volume* of snakes. Take the number of snakes you are imagining and multiply it by ten, then that times ten. Then scream. Snakes on top of snakes. Snakes raining down out of the trees onto the deck of the ship. Snakes up your kilt. Snakes in your hair. Snakes under your jaunty beret.

The mop must have been driving, because Capitaine Hili rushed out onto the deck to pass out torches, which smelled like they had been soaked in vinegar.

"No screaming!" she cried out. "You make screaming, zee snakes panic and start to bite!"

Brilliant. So we were about to be in a world where it rained snakes from above and below, and it was important to *keep very quiet*.

Rí, who is a particularly brave wolfhound, was frozen stiff when the snakes started raining out of the trees. He looked like a statue of a wolfhound.

I scolded Figs in my head for not turning into, say, a mongoose, or even *another kind of snake*, or something useful that might help wrangle the chaos a little bit.

"Ze boat is taking on *beaucoup de* snakes! Too many *beaucoup de* snakes!" cried out Hili, pointing to the bow of the ship, which was sagging very close to the waterline from the weight of all of these snakes.

The ship's steam engine sputtered to a lethargic groan like a robot that did not want to get out of bed for school.

It was abundantly clear how this swamp got its name—our certain death was moments away.

If something didn't happen soon, the *ucky evil* was going under.

The torches would not light, of course. Vinegar doesn't have enough alcohol to burn properly. The torches just smoldered. Everyone with a free hand swatted and tossed snakes overboard as quickly and quietly as they could. But as fast as you could bail snakes, more snakes would slither up over the gunwale or drop from above onto the deck.

Imaginary Dame Judi Dench on my left was doing more than her fair share, as is her style.

I racked my brain for something that would be useful against an unlimited number of snakes. Something more efficient than silently, randomly throwing them. I was on two important vendetti, and I refused to end this mission on the bottom of a river. It also occurred to me that under the snakes the swamp might be full of merrows—also horrible. As I often do, I pictured how *other* Special Unit officers would handle something like this with aplomb.

Even Big Sweaty Jimmy Gibbons got a medal last year for valor, when he was able to give THREE speeding tickets in one month to a headless Dullahan on the M3, which meant twelve points on the Dullahan's license and the confiscation of the hell horse. Of course, because it's the Special Unit, you have to pay the cost of any medals you get, but still. It looks nice on his jacket and he makes a big fuss about it.

Perhaps it is part of being fifteen years old, but the inside of my noggin is a hamster on a Möbius strip, running frantic laps to nowhere and reminding me how everybody else is doing FANTASTIC. *How is everybody else doing so great?*

Then I started to wheeze. It was becoming apparent that I was allergic to some or many of these snakes. When I start to have an allergy attack, my breathing becomes very labored. Less blood flows up into my brain. I start to see things, and sometimes to have MAD thoughts. And just then, as I wheezed, I had my second mad idea of the past twenty-four hours—I asked myself: WWSPD? Which is a little acronym I made up on the spot for *What Would Saint*

Patrick Do? Wasn't it Saint Patrick who banished all these snakes here, singlehandedly? How did he manage to do that in the first place?

How does a young boy with no training in animal wrangling get rid of a lot snakes all at once?

Well, Saint Patrick's big thing was *turning people onto the teachings of Jesus.* Maybe this was worth a shot. While the Boyles are not the most regular church types, I do have a pretty great handle on many of the top Jesus stories. I took a deep breath and in the largest voice I could muster, I told these snakes a little bit about the man from Galilee (from my best recollection).

"And it came to pass that there was a wedding held at Cana, which is in the Bible places. And Jesus went to this wedding with some of his mates: John, Paul, um . . . George!"

Everything stopped. At the very mention of Jesus' name, the snakes turned to face me. The feeling was pure horror.

Then, almost in unison, the snakes rolled their eyes as if to say "not with this stuff again." If snakes could shrug, oh boy—they would have. The stillness passed, and the

snakes hissed at me. I pressed on, just like Saint Patrick would have.

"And they ran out of wine at this wedding, maybe because Jesus brought so many mates who had not RSVP'd, so they didn't have a proper headcount. But Jesus said, 'Don't sweat it, for I am Jesus and I can turn water into wine!' And Jesus did. And this was actually—I think—the first miracle that Jesus performed, probably!?" I preached.

And to my astonishment: This mad plan was working.

Annoyed snakes started slithering away from me. Just a few fled at first, then it was a bona fide panic—as if someone had yelled "JESUS!" in a crowded snake theater. Snakes shot toward the rails of the ship, piling on top of each other trying to get away.

I have no idea why snakes respond like this to stories of Jesus, which are interesting, and usually have *both* magic and a cool moral lesson. Anyway, this was not the time to ask questions; this was the time to preach at snakes who do not want to be preached to. I turned up both my volume and the preachiness to a zillion, peppering my impromptu

sermon with lots of *lo*s and *whence*s and things that sound biblical. Maybe it's the actual word *Jesus* that makes snakes mental, the way that a Ronan Boyle type doesn't like the word *sultry*? We may never know.

"But lo, and whence the wedding guests saw that not only was it wine, it was really top-notch wine. And everyone sayeth so! And they also sayeth, who is this amazing winemaking Jesus bloke? We like this guy! Come asunder and sayeth more things at us. Jesus is our mate!"

"*Bon!* C'est working, Roxanne!" laughed Capitaine Hili. "Encore, encore!" she said as a gaggle of snakes who didn't want to be preached to slithered over her strange feet and off the starboard bow.

"But wait, there's more! Don't go, my legless friends!" I bellowed. Snakes by the bushel were slithering away. "It came whence to passeth that Jesus and his mates were out on a boat in a terrible storm. And there was no way they could get back to the shore, unless—WAIT FOR IT—Jesus walked on top of the water. And lo, he did! And on the way across the water, he turned all of the fish into bread, delicious bread,

and everyone said: Wow, this guy makes wine and bread! Neat, he could open a restaurant, and we would go to it!"

"Why would he change fish into bread, aren't those both food? I think you're mixing up stories," said Log MacDougal, being not at all helpful with her questions while tossing snakes over the horizon with her outstanding throwing arm.

"Just go with it," I said to her out of the corner of my mouth. Then I went back to preaching volume. "And when Jesus came uponeth a fellow who had suffered the terrible ailment of being dead, Jesus said, 'Nope! Not on my watch, wake up, dead fellow!' and the fellow awoken'd, and then they were mates. And then Jesus threw the giant boulder that blocked the entrance to a famous cave, farther than anyone had ever thrown a boulder before." I was now both preaching the good news of the gospel from the best of my recollection and using my shillelagh like a hurley stick to sweep the stragglers off of the deck.

Rí had become unfrozen and was using his snout to

nudge piles of snakes off of the stern. Figs was quietly chewing on Capitaine Hili's unfunny T-shirt, because goats are utterly useless in a situation like this. Figs had often bragged about having "some surprising nasty forms"—this would have been the perfect time for one, Figs!

A short while later, my voice was shot. I was running out of Jesus stories, going through the time he flipped over the tables in the casino, to the story of Christmas itself, with the star and the manger and whatnot. When I ran out of old Jesus stories, I told a story about Jesús Vallejo Lázaro, the defender for the Real Madrid football club.

"Lo, in 2015, Jesús signed with the club for almost six million euros. In four years with the team, he had two goals, which works out to three million euros per goal."

This worked, too! Turns out snakes don't like stories about anybody named Jesus. They kept on departing in droves. A few human minutes later, the ship was cleared.

Hili returned to the wheelhouse and opened up the throttle again. We began to chug around a bend in the river.

The temperature dropped sharply and for a brief time it rained hailstones that looked *and tasted* like garlic knots that you would get at an okay Italian chain restaurant.

The shoreline sharpened again and the River of GLOOM returned to being a proper river. The Swamp of Certain Death was behind us. Along both banks ran tall stone bluffs.

I was flushed and sweaty from all the snake preaching. I was pleased with myself, as I really did remember a lot more about both Jesuses than I expected.

I ate a few of the savory hailstones that landed on the deck, and they really tasted like they'd been made for a large restaurant chain—decent, but with a touch of mass production.

Both Rí and goat-form Figs rubbed their heads against me, showing thanks for my brilliant thinking with the snakes, which as anyone could tell you was really just luck. Ronan Boyle's accidental not at all a superpower. Figs started nibbling on my kilt, and I brushed him off with my shillelagh because I love the kilt almost as much as I love my beret, and goats will chew on anything.

We steamed along all night at a decent clip without incident. At some point Figs turned back into a little man with a hat, and we sat in the wheelhouse eating pressed sandwiches. Capitaine Hili was driving, as the enchanted mop was on a break, smoking its own pipe on the aft deck.

"At daybreak we should make landfall at Wee Burphorn, the last leprechaun outpost on the river before North Ifreann," said Figs. "From Wee Burphorn, we must go a few human hours over land to the wall of the city."

"Ah, *oui*, Wee Burphorn," said Capitaine Hili with a glint in her eye. All I could guess is that there must be some amusing T-shirt shops in Wee Burphorn—as she looked so very pleased.

"I have a few contacts there, we'll see what we can find out about the whereabouts of Captain de Valera and Lily," said Figs. "Get some rest. Once we disembark the ship, this mission will get quite a bit trickier."

Trickier? I'd been almost eaten by carnivorous elves, swam through unicorn poop, had a terrific couple of performances in the Cave of Miracles, how could this get much trickier?

"You'll see," said Figs, answering my question out loud, even though I had only posed it in my mind. (Púcas can occasionally read the minds of people and animals, something that I did not know until this exact moment.)

I had two more pressed sandwiches to reward myself for a big day, then slept for a bit under Rí.

When the engines went quiet, I awoke. I found my glasses and headed up the ladder to the main deck.

With a graceful drift (the mop was driving) we coasted between the piers of the picture-perfect lumber town of Wee Burphorn.

Waiting on the pier was the most beautiful thing I had ever seen.

Chapter Eleven
LILY

Lily!

Chapter Twelve
LILY'S ESCAPE

L ily, my trusted wolfhound partner, was awaiting us on the pier. My heart leaped into my mouth and back down again. I began to cry-laugh or vice versa.

I couldn't help myself—I jumped off the deck of the *ucky evil* and swam the rest of the way through the frigid water. I clambered onto the pier and hugged Lily as hard and as long as anybody ever hugged a humongous dog. She licked my face. Between Lily's saliva and the tears flowing down my cheeks, I must have been quite a spectacle to behold. A few wee dockworkers made rude gestures at us, but I didn't mind. I didn't understand them, anyway.

Twenty human minutes later, we were all tucked into a booth by the blazing fireplace in a pub called the Logger's Rest. Lily and Rí exchanged some significant sniffs—turns out that they are third cousins on Lily's mother's side.

Wee Burphorn is a faerie logging town. Trees are tricked by the wee folk into falling down in the vast forest that lies Upnog of the city. Hundreds of logs a day are then debarked and carved into changelings, harps, and other wooden mischief items. The town is constructed from cedar planks, which gives it the crisp smell of a high-end closet.

Wee Burphorn is home to several hundred Millerchauns, which are not necessarily a *breed* of leprechaun, but a longstanding tradition of faerie woodworkers who shave their beards. This practice is rare for wee folk, but after a thousand years of getting their beards caught in buzz saw blades, the Millerchauns finally got wise.

I sipped on a hot crabapple punch, trying to warm up

from my impulsive leap into the River of GLOOM. Lily's head was nuzzled against my chest as she told the story of her escape from the weegees.

Log translated, as Lily was speaking in the language of the animals, which only sounds like growls to me.

"After the battle at Duncannon Fort, the Red-Eyed Woman and the Bog Man took us through a geata," said Lily via Log. "The captain and I were kept in a vastsack with the harpy and a bunch of other stolen loot—some big old stones with fancy carvings."

Lily paused to lap up some of the soup that the innkeeper had prepared from a wolfhound recipe called "Yesterday's Taco Salad Left in a Saab 900s Turbo."

"The Red-Eyed Woman and the Bog Man are on their way to North Ifreann, for something called the ritual."

"The ritual?" I repeated stupidly, as this is the kind of thing I do.

"She kept saying that the captain will 'serve in the ritual,'" said Lily in the language of the animals. "I was to be ransomed back to the Special Unit for two hundred pounds

of gold, and the release of six of their leprechaun comrades from the Joy Vaults."

"As part of our accord with the wee folk, we do not take hostages, or kidnap each other for ransom!" I shouted, pounding the table with my fist and quoting Wise Young Jim's practices of Irish and Faerie Law class.

"The Special Unit's accord is with the Leprechaun Royal Family in Oifigtown. But the weegees are no better than a gang of thieves." Figs had púca'd himself into a fox, which is an extremely rare but very beautiful púca shape.

"When they opened the vastsack in North Ifreann, I escaped, which took some serious biting of the wee folks' noses and ears and bottoms. The Red-Eyed Woman took a little piece of me with her, too," said Lily via Log, showing off her left ear, which had a small but distinct bite shape taken out of it.

I fumed. The nasty Red-Eyed Woman biting my friend Lily was almost as bad as her kidnapping my friend Lily. I would make her pay for both.

"I ran through the forest for a day and a night. Then this

morning I smelled the river and something particularly stinky coming toward me on the river: a beefie. My friend Detective Ronan Boyle," said Log, translating for Lily.

"But what of the captain?" I asked, shivering, choking back hot crabapple punch, which is actually somewhat disgusting despite its fun-sounding name.

A pall fell across Lily's face.

"I couldn't escape with the captain," said Log, translating. "There was no time. I had to make a split-second decision and fled on my own."

"Muck me clogs!" I said, using leprechaun slang.

Lily's face fell. A somber feeling passed over the Logger's Rest. Then Lily spoke again.

"The captain is to be part of this ritual," Log translated. "A human sacrifice."

And with a trademark Ronan Boyle shriek, I crushed my cup of punch in my bare hand. I could feel the blood in the palm of my hand as the clay bits of the cup scattered to the floor. I'm certain that this reaction was only my concern for Captain de Valera as my ranking officer and a coworker that I respect a great deal and not because of a certain admiration, or . . . not really love, I have for the captain, as I am very to fairly certain that I am not in love with the captain?

Of course I'm not.

My heart was racing and my face was the color of a sour candy that would be called something along the lines of "Electric Strawberry Wipeout."

I squeezed my hand, feeling the blood pulse through my fingers. Oddly, I felt an awfulness in my stomach but nothing at all in my hand.

"The Bog Man has some sort of magical powers. The weegees call him by another name, 'Crumb Crutch' or something. It's hard to tell in the faerie language."

"We must stop this unholy sacrifice," I said, taking off my beret and using it to stop the bleeding in my hand. "To North Ifreann!"

Log and Figs took a moment to finish their pints, which was annoying.

"I'll gather supplies," said Figs. "If we leave now, we can be at the Whinge Wall within a few of your human hours."

Capitaine Hili, who had been dozing by the fireplace, pulled herself up, wobbly, as usual.

"Zis is where I must leave you, beautiful Roxanne Boyle," she said to me, tapping the bottom of her glass to suck the dregs of her red wine, then pinching my cheek. "Tonight je return to EDGE. I wish you *bon chance, mon ami. Bon chance.*" She kissed both of my cheeks and then my lips for longer than you would expect or want. Her breath reeked of pipe smoke and wine sediment. She waved good-bye to the rest of the group, and turned, walking directly into a post and knocking herself out.

"She'll be fine," said Figs. "I give the innkeeper here a little monthly fee to make sure she always makes it back onboard the *ucky evil* before the mop departs without her."

We hustled out of the Logger's Rest and into the fancy-closet-scented air of Wee Burphorn. Figs led the way, with Rí and Lily padding along behind us. The wee folk of town made some rude gestures, all of which seemed to imply getting a body part caught in a buzz saw. Rí said something to Log in the language of the animals, which Log translated.

"Rí says if we could acquire a jaunting car, he and Lily can pull it, and we'd make better time than we would on foot."

"Not a bad idea at all," said Figs, who had turned back into a pig at some point without my noticing.

We headed down the high street of Wee Burphorn. This is a bit of a trick with a group, as the street is less than one meter wide. The streets were never intended for beefies, especially ones in the genre of Log MacDougal.

The market of Wee Burphorn is a vast trading post. It's the last stop for supplies before heading Upnog to North Ifreann.

If it's made of wood and of interest to leprechauns, they sell it in the market at Wee Burphorn: changeling logs, custom harps, clogs and fighting clogs,* guitars, guitars with

---

* The kind of clogs used by leprechauns in fights.

slingshots built into the necks, harps that can also shoot arrows. Enchanted drums that play themselves (the leprechaun version of a drum machine), and flutes and bagpipes of every manner.

The market is also probably the loudest place in Tir Na Nog. Holy cow. I pulled a few spare sets of musking plugs from my utility belt and distributed them around the group to block up our ears. Lily and Rí especially appreciated them, as their hearing was one hundred times more sensitive than any human's.

We passed row after row of wooden wares for sale, including a strange set of wooden eyeballs, hands, legs, teeth, all of which were all secretly flasks for whiskey. Toward the edges of the market were larger items; enchanted butter churns, looms, and what we were seeking—jaunting cars.

Pig-form Figs did some reconnaissance and returned to the group, passing some shredded burlap to Logs from his mouth.

"I've found a jaunting car that the wolfhounds could

pull, but it's being sold by a gancanagh, and I'm afraid that if you see her you will both fall madly in love, so best to put these on," said Figs.

Log and I did as instructed. We were now ear-plugged and blindfolded, which was unsettling. Figs led us both down the street and after a few moments, we were loaded up onto the car. Figs had traded away two of the tiny gold bars on my utility belt, one flask of Jameson whiskey, and all of the items in Figs's CAPTCHA box, including the invisible Ed Sheeran tickets. (I honestly doubt a gancanagh in Wee Burphorn even knew who Ed Sheeran was, but the thought of missing out on free tickets is impossible for a wee person to resist.)

There was a great deal of rustling, clicking, and hitching, and a few minutes later we were rolling along.

"You can lose the blindfolds now," said Figs. Then he screamed this a few times, as we were still wearing earplugs and didn't hear him say this the first couple of times.

I pulled the burlap down to see that we were zipping along in our newly acquired jaunting car, Rí and Lily pulling it briskly. A jaunting car is traditionally meant for one horse, and two wolfhounds are basically the equivalent. If you've never seen a jaunting car, it looks like this:

We zoomed through the striking birch forest that is called Bheithlimbs. The trees are as thin as your fingers and each is a kilometer tall, but the darkness between them was as black as outer space. *Bheith* is a faerie word for *moan*, as when the wind bends the trees in this area, they make a sound as if they are moaning and groaning, with human voices. It's disconcerting until you stop noticing it.

Figs, now a little naked human, was at the reins of the jaunting car, his trusty hat carefully placed in his lap.

"If we keep up like this, we should make good time to the pass, then I have a coyote* who should be able to get us over the wall and into North Ifreann," said Figs.

"Aye," I said, patting the cut in my hand with my beret.

"North Ifreann is a walled city, in the old faerie style," said Figs. "Some say it was to keep unicorns out. But if you ask me, all it did was keep a great deal of evil *in*. It's also the headquarters of your *friends* the weegees, so we'll need to keep a low profile. Beefies aren't welcome."

This struck me as especially menacing, as I have never felt particularly welcome in any part of Tir Na Nog, because, sadly: You have to teach hate.†

---

* Slang for someone who sneaks you across borders.

† I mean you really do, if we don't teach our human children to hate leprechauns at an early age, they will spend the rest of their lives being turned into turnips and plump rabbits. We should have *mandatory* wee folk training in Ireland's elementary schools. Write to your town council!

We rode for a human hour, stopping once to rest the wolf-hounds. The trees of the forest began to change color as we got closer to the Whinge Wall. They were chalky white back near Wee Burphorn, but now they were blood red, like veins shooting up out of the ground.

I could not wait to be out of this place. My hand was throbbing.

It began to snow with huge flakes almost two hundred centimeters wide, each as unique as the print of a lepre-chaun shoe.

Log, Figs, and I huddled together on the jaunting car for warmth. I could see my breath. The steam from Lily's and Rí's noses gave them the appearance of some kind of hell-hounds on the cover of a (human) heavy metal record.

"My coyote at the Whinge Wall is a complicated fellow, but he's precisely what we need for the job," said Figs as the three of us shivered together under a Wee Burphorn sou-venir blanket, which was uncomfortable, as it was made of wood. "He's a good bloke on the inside, I think. Nice enough, if you consider that he's both a werewolf and Scot-tish. So much baggage, so much baggage."

Chapter Thirteen
LAIR OF THE GARYWOLF

We rolled into a lush green hollow that held a hut with a thatched roof. The smell of a peat fire reminded me of the countryside in the human Republic of Ireland. The wailing trees were screaming in harmony around us. Smoke billowed from the hut's chimney. Above us a perfect full moon blasted like a klieg light in the Left End of Nogbottom.

The hut was built partially into the wall of a massive stone structure that rose behind it—the bottom part of the famous Whinge Wall of North Ifreann.

We crossed over a set of stepping-stones through a

small brook of whiskey. I could begin to hear howling from inside the hut. Deep, mournful wails. Figs was now a plump rabbit and was riding upon Rí's back. He held up his paw, making a *shhhh* gesture to the group. We stopped the jaunting car just short of the hut.

"Lay me be, woman!" howled what sounded like a male wolf inside the hut, in the thickest Scottish accent you've ever heard. Seriously, I'm not talking about Glasgow stuff—think Aberdeen. I will transcribe it in this journal as best as my ear could pick it up, but some of it was lost on me.

"Quit your havering, yer oot yer face!" howled what sounded like a female wolf inside the hut.

Log shot me a confused look. "Maybe *you'll* translate for *me* this time, Ronan?" she whispered.

I shrugged.

Figs dismounted and hopped over to the door of the hut, thumping on it with his rabbit foot.

"Haud yer wheest!" growled the shewolf voice from inside.

There was the sound of many padlocks being undone from the other side, and then the door cracked open a pinch. An orange wolf snout poked out and sniffed feverishly at Figs. Then in a twinkling, the snout devoured Figs in one bite.

A female werewolf leaped out the door. She was seven feet tall, with patchy orange fur and massive haunches. Her hands were half human and splattered with bones and bits of meat. Everyone in my group sprang into action or overreaction.

Log tackled the lady werewolf, pinning her to the ground and pulling at her jaws, trying to extract Figs. Log and the werewolf rolled into the whiskey stream—they were well-matched in strength, grappling

ferociously. Log was howling like a lion, *how loud her growl grew!* I thought, thinking my second-ever palindrome.*

"WAIT! STOP! It's your friend Figs and his mates!" I called out, leaping into the brook and trying to pry the she-wolf's jaw open. "It's Horatio Fitzmartin Dromghool inside your mouth! Don't eat him! IT'S YOUR FRIEND FIGS IN RABBIT FORM!"

The lady werewolf picked me up with claws through my beret and threw me five-ish meters into the wall of the hut. Ouch. My kilt flew up, which is always mortifying, and my head suffered a level three bonking.

There was an embarrassing pause. The werewolf stood tall and scanned our faces. She tossed Log aside as if Log were a packing peanut. Then she smacked her lips about,

---

* *STOP. Apologies in advance for the interruption! This is not even close to a palindrome. On behalf of the Special Unit of Tir Na Nog, and the Republic of Ireland, our sincere apologies. As a nation we have failed young people like Ronan Boyle by letting them think that palindromes are some manner of AWKWARD ALLITERA-TION. Teach your children about palindromes—WRITE YOUR TOWN COUNCIL. Your man in Killarney, Finbar Dowd.*

as if she recognized the flavor inside. She pulled a spit-covered Figs out of her mouth. She held him by his rabbit haunches and eyed him suspiciously.

"If'n this be the real Figs Dromghool, where the devil is his 'at at?" she growled, a bit of hot werewolf spit dripping from her maw.

"Where's his AT–AT?" I asked aloud, like an eejit, thinking of the large stomping vehicles of the Empire and how useless they were against an ordinary tow cable on a snow speeder.

"His 'AT! THE 'AT THAT FIGS ALWAYS WEARS ON HIS 'EAD, YA NUMPTY!"

"Oh, his *HAT?!*" I said, finally understanding her lavish Scottish accent. "It's right here somewhere! I promise!" I scrambled into a pile of supplies up on the jaunting car. At some point Figs's famous hat had fallen off, likely when he sprouted his rabbit ears. I finally found it underneath several jars of hot pickles that Figs had purchased without my knowledge. I held out the hat, waving it like a surrender flag, and cautiously approached the werewolf.

"There it is! His famous hat!" I said, tiptoeing toward them.

"Right'o. There you have it. Good ol' Figs here, shape of a hare!" said Figs through his adorable rabbit teeth. "Never know what Figs will become, even got a few scary forms! But not today, ol' Rabbit Figs, NOT FOR EATING, barely enough to make a soup, Freya!"

The shewolf burst into a hacking laugh. "Figs, ya old bass!" She beamed, now recognizing him. She wiped him off under her furry armpit. "Fit like?"

"Nae bad!"* giggled Figs as they embraced.

"Yer a sight for sore eyes, and look at mae self, with me bum hanging out the window like a numby," said the werewolf whose name was, apparently, Freya.

"Bum out the window" is a Scottish expression of embarrassment. I'm not sure if this happened to some famous Scot and then became an expression, but it's worth keeping in your head and remembering. There's been many

---

* *How are you* and *not bad* to very, very Scottish types.

a time my bum has been out a proverbial window, but I had no words to explain it until now.

"Let's have a hello to yer mayyytes." Freya the were-wolf went around sniffing everyone aggressively, including the wolfhounds, who looked a bit put off by it. Wolfhounds are related to regular wolves, but they are NOT related to werewolves, who are mostly Scots. Of course, some wolf-hounds are related to werewolves by marriage.

"I've come for yer lad, Gary. Got some business to sort out with the weegees in North Ifreann," said Figs. "Must get over the Whinge Wall tonight."

Freya made a *tsk, tsk* sound, as if to suggest that going up the wall into North Ifreann was a bad idea—which it surely was.

"Come aught the cauld," said Freya, licking her maw and stretching. "I'll try to roust the lad!"

She ducked into the hut, calling out, "MOVE YER ARSE, ye've company, lad!"

The sitting room of the hut was cozy indeed. The fur-nishings were mostly entry-level IKEA stuff from the human realm, which made it seem like this was probably a furnished rental. A peat fire burned in a potbelly stove. The unforgettable aroma of werewolf musk came off of, well—everything. Without making a big fuss, I popped my musking plugs into my nose for a respite.

The bones of someone or something were strewn about the floor of the hut. While werewolves have tried to adapt to modern times, they still hunt the moors at night, feasting on the living. And yes—it can make them feel depressed and bloated afterward.

Luckily for us in the human Republic, air pollution has made clear nights with a visible full moon scant. Many modern werewolves don't even change into their wolf forms anymore. It's yet another effect of climate change that the government and the big conglomerates don't want you to know about. If you don't believe in air pollution, ask the werewolves. Unsafe air quality in the human realms has led many werewolves to permanently relocate in Tir Na Nog, which has stricter environmental laws than ours, and juicer things to devour at night.

Since it's always a full moon over North Ifreann, lots of unemployed werewolves have created a little suburb of dens and lairs around the eastern (or ? direction on faerie maps) section of the wall. A sudden boom in werewolves can be tough on an economy, especially for a forest with lots of young male werewolves like Gary who have no particular job skills or motivation.

Gary was lounging on an old plaid sofa, sipping an Irn-Bru (a popular orange–flavored soda with caffeine from the human country of Scotland). Gary was bopping his head, plucking the strings of an out–of–tune guitar, attempting to play along with the solo part on the Waterboys' "Fisherman's Blues," which was spinning on a turntable so brand–new that it *seemed* like it must have been stolen from humans.

I can't say if Gary was much of a specimen of a werewolf. He remains one of only two I have ever met, including his mum, Freya. Gary was three meters tall, dangerously thin, almost gaunt, with a partial spiderweb tattoo that rose from his neck onto the lower part of his face.

His guitar playing was in the bottom five I had ever

heard. His massive claws didn't help much. This seemed very much like the first time he'd ever even tried to play a guitar. Let's hope that it was.

Gary's face was partially human, with a shock of orange fur all around it like a lion's mane. He nodded hello as Figs hopped toward him, dropping the guitar with a terrible clatter, tugging at his ripped human pants, which must have shredded themselves when he turned into a werewolf at some point.

"Figs Dromghool! Fit like?" said Gary, with a smile that revealed some poorly maintained teeth. Why Gary wore a flesh-colored Band-Aid over his left eye we may never know. I certainly wasn't going to ask about it.

"Gary, you ol' bass!" replied Figs, hugging Gary's leg.

Gary scooped Figs up in his werewolf arms, which displayed many tattoos between the patchy fur. Gary had even more tattoos than Log MacDougal, who until this point had the most I had ever seen. The visible ones on Gary read SCOTLAND FOREVER, WEREWOLVES FOREVER, and one seemed to be an image of a one-liter bottle of Irn-Bru.

Wow. Gary was the real deal. You'd be hard-pressed to find a more Scottish werewolf than him.

"Care for a bit o' ginger, Figs?" asked Gary, offering his Irn-Bru.

"Aye!" said Figs.

Gary poured some Irn-Bru directly into Figs's rabbit mouth. Figs guzzled it down and then let out a gigantic burp, scratching his foot against his chin. An orange cloud of sugar and caffeine passed over the room. My eyes fought to stay open against it.

"Ye lot lookin' to get up over the Whinge Wall, then?" said Gary.

"Aye," said Figs. "Allow me to introduce Detective Ronan Boyle of the Garda Special Unit of Tir Na Nog."

I bowed, doffing my beret, which is one of my favorite things to do when meeting people and/or things. "At your service," I said, resetting my beret in the jaunty way I prefer with the Special Unit logo pointing to the left.

"Ain't he a wee stuck up?" said Gary, laughing at me

harder than was appropriate. "You just wee stuck up, boyo. Barely a lad! They couldn't send a ladybug instead?"

I laughed this off awkwardly as Gary gave me an amusing but forceful punch in the arm, but really it served as a great reminder that it wasn't *just me* who thought myself unqualified to be here, at least it was EVERYONE who thought that! UNANIMOUS THAT I AM A FRAUD! *Try to smile? Playing along with the joke. Why am I so sweaty? Why did I high-five Yogi Hansra that one time? Does she think about it as often as I do?* I attempted to act official.

"And these are my partners, Lily, WSU; Rí, WSU; and Log MacDougal, cadet, accidentally raised as a log by the wee folk," I said.*

"Aye, it happens," said Gary giving a hug to Log MacDougal.

Log and Gary scanned each other's tattoos for a moment, mumbling things like *oh, nice* and *fit like.* In many ways, they seemed like long-lost soulmates.

---

* WSU = Wolfhound Special Unit.

"Bit o' the ginger, Log MacDougal?" asked Gary as he scratched his belly (which seemed to be VERY itchy), holding out his can of Irn-Bru to Log. Log took a huge swig of it, pleased, then passed it to me. It was evident from the sound of the can that this was now mostly orange backwash.

"Nae, I'm all fit like—cheers," I said, attempting to use some Scottish slang. "Time is against us, and we've got to stop a human sacrifice on the other side of the wall in North Ifreann."

"So, ye are heading over the wall?" said Gary. "How you plannin' that? 'Tis a right muckfest these days getting up the wall."

"Well, that's where *you* come in, Gary," I said, confused, as we were only meeting Gary to be our coyote over the wall. There was literally and figuratively no other reason we were here talking to Gary in this musky hut.

"Aye. Brilliant," said Gary, swishing that last backwash bit of Irn-Bru around in his mouth to savor the flavor. "When ye all plannin' to go?"

Gary stood there, a dim look in his magnificent green eyes. I have no idea how he wasn't understanding all of this.

"Um. We need to go right exactly now, in fact—a little while ago would have been ideal," I said, trying to be as firm and clear as possible.

"Oi, so ye want to leave right now? Well, there's nae danger of that," said Gary, crushing the Irn-Bru can in his huge claws. "I've already got a paying customer tonight. Sorry luvs, nae can take you."

"You've—already got a customer? But we can pay whatever you ask! Let me show you my BeefCard," I protested. "I'm sure your other client won't mind us joining in on his or her excursion up the wall?"

"Nae, except—he might actually," said Gary softly, checking over his shoulder. "Not the nicest bloke, if you get my drift. Bit of a trick, in fact. Nasty old beefie. Aye, here he comes now from the loo."

A toilet flushed in the back room.

If the next look on my face were a painting in a museum, it would be called *Portrait of Irish Teen Silently Screaming.*

I screamed, silently, and then out loud.

From the darkness in the back of the hut something pointy was born into the light. I recognized it in an instant. It was the tip of a very nice umbrella. *My umbrella!* The very one I had left behind when I fled Lord Desmond Dooley's art gallery on Henrietta Street.

Clutching at the handle end of it was the twisted hand of the man himself—Lord Desmond Dooley. My nemesis. The man who looks like a gargoyle with the flu. The man who framed my parents for stealing the mummy called the Bog Man and let them rot in Mountjoy Prison for his crime. A man I despise with every molecule of my body, from my toes to my optional beret.

His face was as pointy as ever. He was wearing a leather cape, with gloves and tinted pince-nez with dark glass, as if he had somehow had an *evil makeover* since I last saw him.

Dooley limped across the room toward me. He poked the tip of my umbrella into my sternum.

"Young masssster Boyle," he hissed. "Congratulations, I read in the newspapers that your parents have escaped from Mountjoy Prison with their gang. This must be a great comfort to you, boyo. Mum and Da, no longer locked up for something they didn't do."

If anyone could describe Lord Desmond Dooley as *giggling*, that's what happened next. A hollow chortle came from his throat as the corners of his mouth pulled up.

"*Lord* Desmond Dooley," I spit out with disdain and with emphasis to show that I knew that "Lord" was his actual first name, not a title. With my left hand I quietly unclicked my shillelagh from the hooks on my back, ready to thump him directly across his bald noggin. "For the record, my parents are in *two different gangs!*"

"I've been a day or so behind you since you left Killarney, Boyle. I almost caught up to you in the Steps mountains, but the Free Men of the Pole delayed me for a bit." He gestured to his foot, which was wrapped up tightly in Christmas paper. "I'm afraid the Free Men made some pass-arounds from my toes before I was able to escape."

I shuddered. This was disgusting. And even for

cannibal-type monsters like the Free Men: What kind of pass-arounds could you make from Dooley's foul little toes? There's not enough garlic bread crumbs or jalapeños in the world to make Dooley toes palatable.

"A far darrig named Ricky in Bad Aonbheannach told me that I arrived only an hour after you escaped the Cave of Miracles," said Dooley. "I must have made up some time against you in the Bheithlimbs to get here to the wall before you. Well, sorry to spoil yer fun, but this is where your journey ends, lad."

Dooley pulled an antique bronze-age dagger from his sleeve and twirled it.

I pulled my shillelagh using Yogi Hansra's famous Hansra Pull, a method of drawing and cracking the opponent's jaw that is so foolproof that she named it after herself.

I missed.

Not because the move was executed poorly, but because before I could thump him, Log had already hoisted Dooley in one of her famous wedgies.

Log giggled psychotically as Dooley dangled from her stupendous arm. He tried to swat at her with the dagger *and* my umbrella, but only connected with the air.

Gary's eyes lit up as he watched Log dangle a full-grown man by his underpants.

"That's my kind of girl!" said Gary, looking a bit smitten. Log blushed, which I had never seen her do before.

"Boyle, ya filthy devil!" said Dooley, now in the sad voice of a man being held aloft by his underwear.

I didn't respond. Gary's mum, Freya, broke the silence:

"So ye've all met, then?" she said, passing Gary a fresh liter of Irn-Bru.

"As a point of fact, we have," I said, twirling my shillelagh and employing the best scowl a Ronan Boyle type can muster. "This is Mister Dooley. Art thief, smuggler, and framer of innocent persons! He's an accomplice of the weegees and wanted for questioning in the disappearance of Captain Siobhán de Valera."

From the sporran on my kilt I pulled out two weerrants.

One for the Red-Eyed Woman, and one for the Bog Man himself. These are arrest warrants issued for the wee folk, signed by Deputy Commissioner Finbar Dowd. They are somewhat pointless, as no faerie folk would ever recognize their legitimacy. But waving the weerrants in Dooley's face added gravitas to the moment, so I stuck with it.

Freya threw up her claws in disgust.

"This is why I don't like doin' this type o' business," Freya howled. "I pay to keep up this place, and yer nothing but a boil on me bum, Gary. I'm the one buyin' yer clover and Irn-Bru. And ye missin' the toilet every time!"

"And yeeee with yer *havering*!" howled Gary in her face.

Gary and his mum began snapping at each other, growling and biting like you might see ordinary wolves fighting for dominance on a Nature Channel show. Soon they were a blur of orange fur and spilled Irn-Bru.

"Perhaps we should take this outside!" yelled Figs, now a naked little man in a hat, forgetting to cover his bits.

Oh dear. If only I could unsee this.

The whole scenario was bonkers. Log kept Dooley in a weaponized wedgie as we all inched our way out of the hut.

"Not one false move, Dooley," I said, "or you're like the antiques you sell: history." (This sounded brilliant in my head but came out a bit clunky from my mouth.)

Chapter Fourteen
CROM CRUACH

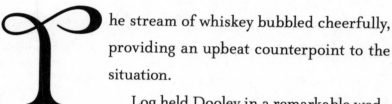he stream of whiskey bubbled cheerfully, providing an upbeat counterpoint to the situation.

Log held Dooley in a remarkable wedgie. Even by Log's standards, this was one for the books. Rí and Lily were at my sides, ready to pounce if Dooley tried anything funny.

Human-form Figs's famous hat was now covering his bits, which made things less *oh dear*–ish.

Gary and Freya had found a brief truce. They were

grooming each other like wolves, finding itchy parts to scratch. In the moonlight, I could see that Freya also had a lot of tattoos and that most of them were awful.

"Am I under arrest, boyo?" asked Dooley, trying to burn a hole in me with his eyes.

"Perhaps," I replied as I paced, my eyes in a laser lock with Dooley. I clicked on my torch and pointed it in his face. "And it's not 'boyo,' it's Detective Ronan Boyle, thank you very much." I twirled my torch because that's what Captain de Valera would do, as she is amazing at these types of things. Side note: No, I do not think I am in love with the captain, but sometimes romantic thoughts do flash through my head.

"I do not recognize the authority of the Special Unit!" barked Dooley as he made a little snort from his nose, sending evil snot into the air.

"Dooley, I should feed you to the wolfhounds," I bluffed, dramatically.

"Ha! You wouldn't hurt a rabbit, Boyle. No offense to your púca friend."

"Careful, I have a few nasty shapes you haven't met yet," said Figs.

"There's one detail that you're wrong about in all of this unpleasantness. I am not your enemy, Boyle," said Dooley.

Log switched hands, moving Dooley to a right-hand wedgie hold. (Log is ambidextrous—she has no dominant hand).

"Please—believe me! I'm on your side now! The Red-Eyed Woman betrayed me," said Dooley. "Fine, maybe I did steal the Bog Man from your mum and da. And yes, I had planned to sell him to a buyer in Dubai for a private museum, which is illegal. And sure, I would have been rich beyond my wildest dreams. And fine, I've been up to no good for most of me life—but now, I'm just trying to get the Bog Man back. Same as you, Boyle."

I scowled, doing my best to not get lured in by this nefarious not-a-lord.

"I could even help you if you'd let me, Boyle. All of the things I did . . . so foolish. But that was before I knew the Bog Man's true identity."

Tears welled up in Dooley's eyes. I wish I could say that he was faking, but after some really tight shows in the Cave of Miracles, I know how hard it is to cry on cue. These were real tears streaming down Dooley's face.

"The Red-Eyed Woman and her weegees came sniffing around before I could close the deal with my Dubai associate," he said, still sniffling. "At the time I didn't think much of it, we did some transactions from time to time. Mostly I'd sell 'em stray harpies and old brass spears, sacred knickknacks. But this time they'd come for the Bog Man and the next thing I know—pickle spray in me face! Brass knuckles to me noggin! Bites to me knees! The weegees say I work for them now. They whacked the stuffing out of me— you have no idea what that's like, Boyle. Nasty little devils, those weegees. I'm not with them, not nae more, I swear!"

I had a specific idea of what a beating from the weegees was like, as I'd been on the receiving end of both bites and whacks from the Red-Eyed Woman and her gang at Duncannon Fort. I still had the bruises to show for it.

"Blarney!" I blurted. "This is a web of blarney because you're outnumbered and want to escape in one piece."

Dooley shook his head. At this point he'd been in a wedgie for as long as anyone on record.

"Boyle, I thought the Bog Man was just some trinket when I agreed to sell him. A mummy for display, stiff as a board. Dead as a doornail, for nigh on four thousand years. I didn't know who he really is. But now I do."

"And who is he, your grandmum?" I said, acting tough, using a snarky tone that's not my usual style at all.

A cloud passed over Dooley's face. Everything dimmed, as if someone had turned down the moon above us.

"The Bog Man is called Crom Cruach," said Dooley heavily.

"And Crom Cruach is . . . what exactly? I asked.

"Ye don't know? O'course ye don't know, schools these days, pfffft!" said Dooley with a sniff.

Then he checked over his shoulder. His voice became a whisper, as if he didn't want the moaning trees to hear us. "Crom Cruach is one of the old gods of Ireland. Before Saint Patrick came and got rid of them and the snakes. Some say Crom Cruach was the sun god, but he demanded the darkest form of worship. Crom Cruach wanted human sacrifice."

A zap ran up my spine as if I had stepped on a jellyfish.

"Crom Cruach! That's the name. Not Crumb Crutch," said Log (translating for Lily, who was barking like mad).

"You're not chasing after a mummy, Ronan Boyle—you're chasin' after a god," said Dooley.

My shillelagh dropped to the forest floor without a sound.

Everyone stood frozen for a long moment. My mind raced.

I had been a detective now in the Special Unit for approximately five days. Most of my career was spent in training. My last big case had been the theft of SOME WINE. I had barely graduated from Tin Whistle for Beginners with the lowest passing grade. I am fairly sure I cannot recite the Recruit's Pledge properly. No part of my resume made me qualified to be in hot pursuit of an undead Irish god. There were far more qualified officers in the Special Unit. This was precisely the kind of case that should be handled by Commissioner McManus himself!

As I am always close to the truth in this journal, I will let you know that I wet my first set of underpants a little bit. I'm not proud of it, but these are the facts as they transpired.

"My parents dug up—a god?" I stammered.

"More like the devil himself. They didn't know what he was. How could they have known? I didn't know until the Red-Eyed Woman shows up so interested. She and her gang start calling him 'Crom Cruach.' They start worshipping the geezer right there in my back room," said Dooley. "The wee folk live a long time, boy. The Red-Eyed Woman and Crom Cruach go way back. She and her mates are the last of his devotees. The Cult of Crom Cruach they call themselves."

My trembling hand scrawled out: *Cult of Crom Cruach* in my notebook. It rang the vaguest bell in my head. But from where? Then it hit me: CROM CRUACH! Precisely who Brian Bean warned me about in my dream or possibly not-a-dream!

"Red-Eyed Woman pulls out a book of spells in Goídelc—the old language—and puts one on Crom Cruach called Finnegan's Wake or some such. She says this incantation and throws decent whiskey over his face. Next thing I know, he sits right up on the table, alive—or undead. Oh, his breath—something I won't soon forget. The morning breath of four thousand years. I swear on me mum's grave that it's true," said Dooley. "And yes, I had a mum—Fiona was her name. Same name as yer mum, Boyle."

"Don't try to curry sympathy from me while you clutch my very nice umbrella, you scoundrel!" I said.

I yanked away the umbrella, sticking it between my belt and my kilt and accidentally poking my thigh so, so hard. I would not lose my nice umbrella again.

I had never doubted myself more than this moment, and keep in mind: Self-doubt is like my full-time hobby. I was not cut out for these type of vendetti.

I knew what I should do: OVERTHINK MY NEXT MOVE for several arduous minutes while a flop sweat seeps from my beret.

But then a clear thought rang out like a bell in my worried mind. I decided that if I really was an imposter, as it always felt like, I should at least be an imposter of someone smarter and braver than me.

I decided to become an imposter of Captain de Valera. And the captain doesn't think—she acts.

"Lord Desmond Dooley, in the name of the Commissioner of the Special Unit, you are under arrest for conspiracy, abetting in a kidnapping, transfer of stolen goods and/or mummies. Cuff him, Cadet MacDougal," I pronounced firmly, just like the captain would.

Dooley misted snot at me from his last remaining weapon—his nose.

Log dropped Dooley out of the wedgie and cuffed him to my wrist.

"Gary, oh brave werewolf!" I bellowed, adding the word *brave* to win him over. "You shall deliver us over the wall of North Ifreann this very night!"

"Tonight? Tonight's nae good for me." Gary shrugged, licking a part of his werewolf body that I will not describe to you, as you are decent people. "I've got a thing."

I paced in the style of the captain, trying to think of a way to convince Gary to take us up the wall right away.

"But! Ye shall be rewarded, brave Gary. In exchange for your assistance tonight . . . um . . . you shall receive a

full pardon for all those crimes ye have committed in the human country of Scotland! They shall be wiped from your permanent record, forever, in perpetuity, ipso-facto. I, Detective Ronan Boyle, am authorized to make this deal per the accord between the Special Unit of Tir Na Nog, and our friends at the Poileas Sìthichean."*

Gary fidgeted and scratched himself for a moment. A complex series of guilty looks moved across his face, like Doppler news radar showing the next five days of emotions.

I should let you in on a small secret: I did not have evidence of any crimes committed by Gary in the human country of Scotland. This was a HUNCH. No werewolf with that many tattoos and that much Irn-Bru in his bloodstream DID NOT have a thing or two on their record, right?

---

* The Poileas Sìthichean is the Scottish counterpart to the Garda Special Unit of Tir Na Nog. They are headquartered in what looks like an old tin of Pringles under a bridge in Kelvingrove Park, Glasgow. The Poileas Sìthichean deal with Scottish faerie folk who are both abundant and fiercely proud of their heritage. If you're on holiday in Glasgow: DO NOT attempt to visit the office, as it's guarded by a cat sìth, which is a demonic cat the size of a cow, and also by two human Glaswegians—and Glaswegians are *not* to be trifled with.

I waited, bluffing, trying to present myself as the very serious detective I might one day be.

"Ah, think, Gary, all the bad deeds ye done, expunged forever," said Freya as she nuzzled him, getting some of her copious blue eyeshadow on his chest fur.

The gambit paid off. Gary extended his claws to me.

"Fer Mum, yes. I'll do it. And I have yer word, then, beefie. My crimes will be explunged?" asked Gary, mispronouncing *expunged*. "Keep in mind, some o' them beefies I ate in Girvan was numbies who weren't no good use to anybody outside of me belly anyways."

"You have my word, Gary the Werewolf," I said, shaking his jittery paw. "Now, there's no time to waste—we have a sacrifice to stop."

"And nothing to wear," added Figs, who had nothing to wear except his hat.

Chapter Fifteen

UP THE WHINGE WALL

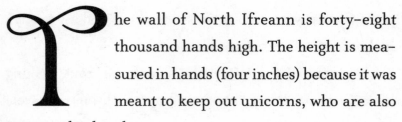he wall of North Ifreann is forty-eight thousand hands high. The height is measured in hands (four inches) because it was meant to keep out unicorns, who are also measured in hands.

The wall is made of lava stones, which are overgrown in a thin black moss that makes the wall as slippery as a freshly resurfaced ice rink. Legend (and Gary) says that a euro coin dropped from the top of the wall will take a whole human minute to land at the bottom. It's a long way down. And then you're out a euro, so don't ever do this.

Some of the stones used to construct the wall are enchanted with leprechaun spells, so they have a tiny but annoying power, which makes mounting the wall quite tedious.

"Some o' the stones bite," explained Gary, chugging yet another (his fifth? sixth?) Irn-Bru of the evening. "Some'll boke* on ya, which is foul. Many folks lost a good few fingers. But by far, the worst part of the wall is . . . the *whinge-in'*."

It turns out that many of the stones in the wall complain, or *whinge* in Scottish slang. This gives the wall its nickname: the Whinge Wall.

"They'll be whinging about their miserable job being rocks in a wall, but ye gotta stick yer foot right in their stupid mouth, then jump out before they bite ya," explained Gary. "The stones don't *love* being part of a wall, so that explains all the whinging. Don't listen to 'em. I don't like my job neither, but you don't hear me whingin' about it."

Gary went around and picked up each member of our

---

* Scottish for vomit.

team and considered their weight for a moment. To say that Gary was ten times stronger than Log might be an underestimate. He set us all back down in a line, from heaviest to lightest, doing some kind of math in his head.

From a filthy sack, Gary pulled out some ropes and hooks. He began to fasten the ropes around our midsections, tethering us together. Log, being solid muscle, was at the top of the line. Following her were Lily, Rí, me, then Dooley (handcuffed to me), then Figs at the end. I did *not* like the fact that Dooley would be below me on the climb, especially when I was in a kilt.

"You can't hoist me up the wall in handcuffs! This is unethical!" Dooley complained.

"Quit yer *whing*in'!" I said, using my new favorite verb.

Gary's claws were shaking as he fastened the ropes around my middle. Now that it was happening, I had deep reservations about Gary being our coyote. He didn't seem up to the task in any way. And he was so, so twitchy.

"This may seem like an obvious question, but *why* exactly

do we need a werewolf to get up the wall? Is it the claws, or . . . some talent that Gary hasn't yet displayed? There must be something I'm missing, right?" I whispered to Figs.

"The claws help, for sure," said Figs. "Very few creatures have claws that will take a deeper bite into the Whinge Wall than the werewolf. But the *Scottish* werewolf turns out to be one of the only creatures that can climb the wall, and the main reason is: attitude."

"Attitude?" I repeated, confused.

"Aye," said Figs. "And I'm not even sure it's the were-wolf part that matters. Being Scottish is the key. The Scots take no muck off of anybody. They're ready to fight and kill for any reason or no reason at all. Scots are the only thing that can make it over the wall because, well—*who would stop them?* They'll give you a *Glasgow smile* across yer mug as soon as look at ya. Poor Gary. Just a product of his environment."

Figs gestured toward Gary, who was cracking his knuckles, ready for a fight, a wild, faraway look in his sad green eyes. He had tossed away his last can of Irn-Bru and was now having a swig off of something called

Buckfast Tonic, which is a strong wine with caffeine for some Scottish reason.

I noticed that under the bits of fur, Gary's human face had two upturned scars by the corners of his mouth (a street-fighting scar called the Glasgow smile). While I was noticing, Gary polished off a second bottle of Buckfast in record time.

"YOU CAN NAEEE KILL THE GARYWOLF! NAE KILL THE GARYWOLF!" screamed Gary, with a sadness in his eyes that I will never be able to fully convey to you. My young heart broke. Poor Gary, trying to do right by his mum. Trying to work on his recreational guitar playing. Trying to be a decent werewolf, but caught up in an endless cycle of unemployment, violence, Irn-Bru, and low self-esteem.

The reason that Gary the Werewolf was uniquely qualified to get us over the wall is simply because Gary's life is violent nihilistic tilt at every available windmill.

(Note: In the intense wave of sadness that washed over my mind, I flashed back to Pierre the far darrig. He was still a prisoner of the Free Men of the Pole, some of whom had eaten Dooley's toes. It's likely Pierre was still playing dead in a stocking high in the snowy steeps. I really would go back for him at some later date, after all of this was settled and Captain de Valera was safe again. I'm certain I would return for him! And I will! Poor thing. I would put a pin in this for now, but certainly NEVER FORGET PIERRE! Probably never! Pinning this idea for now, but certainly not something I will forget soon.)

What was I writing about?

Oh, right: Gary was breaking my heart and apparently about to lead us up a slick forty-eight-thousand-hands-high wall of complaining, barfing rocks. Gary was amped to the gills on multiple cans of Irn-Bru and a fortified wine that was adding to his remarkable Scottishness. If a were-wolf could then turn into something more frightening than itself, Gary would have at this moment. His eye that was not under a Band-Aid was twitching from all the caffeine.

"Thank ye, beefie," said Freya, lightly digging her claws into my biceps. "Gary's a good boy, and keep in mind, in werewolf years, he's only five."

Oooof. That was a genuine bummer. Werewolf years are approximate to dog years, so Gary was only thirty-five years old. This was really the most distressing news of the day because he looked like a badly preserved fifty-five to sixty years old.

Gary stepped toward the wall, eyeing it like an old foe. "Me claws will find purchase. I'll be doin' most all the work. The best ye can do is resist the urge to help me. My motto: *No whingin, no mingers, or our tatties are over the side.**

"Figs, yer at the *coo's tail*,† so no shape-shifting into one of yer big nasty forms," added Gary. "I can nae pull the weight of your biggies!"

"I'll nae try to shape-shift," said Figs, shrugging, "but as ye know, it's not my decision!"

---

* *No complaining, no dirty people, or our potatoes will be gone.* This makes sense to Scottish people and werewolves.

† Scottish for *the end*, as in a cow's tail.

"More than anything, all of you: Keep the heid," said Gary, meaning *keep your head about you.*

Everyone nodded except Dooley, who sniffed. I poked him with my nice umbrella right in his bony shin, then I instantly felt bad as I watched him hop on his Christmas-wrapped foot. (Seriously, the Free Men would barely even have gotten any meat off of Dooley's toes, except maybe the big one. Did they put wing sauce on them? Do they even have access to a deep fryer? This was a disgusting puzzle that would haunt me for years to come.)

Gary crouched, burped out Irn-Bru, and took a massive leap up into the air that yanked our charm bracelet of heroes and villains behind him thirty meters up the wall.

There was an ear-splitting crack as his claws cut into the lava stones. My chin smacked against the wall and I bit my tongue. I was about to yelp, but I did not want to be cut loose for whinging.

Before I could recover, Gary leaped again, tugging us all behind him like potatoes on a string.

The ride was dreadful. The passengers on the rope

below me weren't that heavy per se, just Dooley and Figs, but the handcuffs connecting me to Dooley were starting to cut a mark into my wrist.

We continued up like this for a bit. It was not a graceful climb. Most if not all parts of my body would be injured on the ride. We were making brisk upward progress until we met our first whinging rock. I was not prepared for how passive-aggressive these rocks could be.

"Oh, hi. Don't even worry about me, human guy," said the whinging rock, with his sad rock face. The rock took a bite into my sporran, holding me there. Through his clenched teeth he complained ad nauseam.

"Did you know that I was carved and stuck here as a child. Imagine: *as a child*. Wish I'd gotten to be at Mum's funeral, but you can't win 'em all. It's fine because I never really met her."

Oh boy. This rock was a real bummer. I tried to pull my sporran free, but his teeth had a terrific grip, despite his whinging.

"Don't ye listen to that whingin' minger!" howled Gary from above.

"Go, go on up. Leave me here!" mumbled the rock with a mouthful of sporran. "I should have been dead by now anyway. Maybe I am? Maybe being part of this wall is punishment for some crimes I did in a past life. Why is this me instead of you? This could have been either of us. Ah, go on with ya. LEAVE ME HERE. Leave me here to die!"

The rock wept, soaking my sporran with tears and moss snot. Ugh.

"PAY NAE MIND TO THE WHINGIN'!" howled Gary. "Get yerself free, Boyle, or I'll cut ye loose right now!"

I did not want to be cut loose. I unclicked the metal hooks of my sporran. I loved that sporran, but I couldn't let it hold us all back with this rock, who made some decent points. That's the real danger of the Whinge Wall—not *all* of the complaints are far-fetched, and some of them hit home.

We pressed upward for some time, my nice umbrella cutting a mark into my side, the handcuffs into my wrist.

By the time we reached the very top, three of my ribs were cracked from the rope and one from my nice umbrella poking into me. I should have jettisoned the

umbrella, but as I had vowed to get it back, I could not part with it again.

By the top of the wall we had escaped complaints from many of the rocks; gripes about the weather, about the moss growing on their faces, but mostly about *politics*. If you've ever been to a family gathering with an uncle who is underinformed and overopinionated: that's what climbing the Whinge Wall is like. Direct quotes from some of these rocks were:

"The weegees are very fine people who love Tir Na Nog more than other faerie folk."

"Unicorns should have to carry papers that say they are jerks."

"The only good far darrig is the one cooking in your stewpot."

"Leprechauns are thieves." (This one is probably true, no argument here.)

"Queen Moira's plans to make humans into sausages was NOT EXTREME ENOUGH."

It was a dizzying, awful ride up the wall—but it was the *ideas* I heard on the way up that really made me queasy.

Chapter Sixteen
THE DEVIL'S PINCUSHION

top the wall, Gary disconnected the ropes that had bound us together.

Everyone was battered and bruised, reeling from the terrible complaints of rocks who probably haven't read an actual book in years.

Log and Rí licked paws, cleaning the moss out of their pads. We crossed over the top section of the wall, which was made with broken glass set into the mortar—one final low-tech discouragement to visitors.

My knee protectors saved the day. I was carrying Figs on my back and pulling Dooley along by the handcuffs.

I missed my sporran, especially because it ties together with my beret so nicely.

We peered over the lip of the inner part of the wall to see North Ifreann. True to its name in the language of the faeries, it looked like a fiery hellscape—a place where the wee folk are sent to pay for their crimes. I could hear screams coming from three distinct points in the city.

North Ifreann is a pit both literally and figuratively. Fish oil smoke puffed out from a thousand chimneys down below. The city is a puzzle of alleyways zigzagging up toward the Shousting Dome in the center of town.

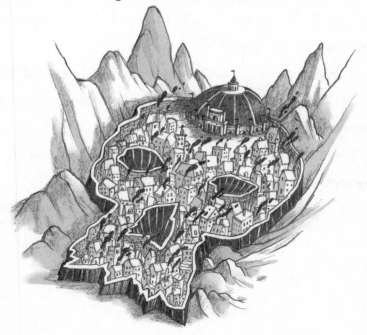

Something big (harpies?) were flying about in the air, but they were only visible by the soot they displaced as they passed.

From above, the city looks remarkably like a human skull, with the Shousting Dome as the skull cap.

"North Ifreann. Nae a nice place to live, nae a nice place to visit. *Too scary for the Gary.* This is where I leave ye," said Gary. "I hope ye'll be as good as yer word, beefie. I want to be able to go back to human Scotland, without a bunch of hassle about: *Hey, what about all these evidence bones with your bite radius on 'em, Gary? Where are the rest of the bodies, Gary! Look, we got yer DNA, Gary! Confess, Gary, confess!* Blah blah blah . . . I'm so sick of it all playing out in me heid over and over!"

"Right! I shall, Gary," I said, now a bit nervous about what I had promised. "You'll never have to worry about that silly stuff again. I'm on top of it."

(Note: I would have to remember to really contact my counterparts in Glasgow and try to get a pardon for whatever Gary had actually done, some of which sounded

QUITE serious, included the eating of humans in Girvan, which in Ireland would be eighteen months in the Joy Vaults.)

I would not forget this promise, as I would probably never forget Pierre, up in the Steps!

Gary leaped off the wall, humming the Proclaimers' song "500 Miles."

I was concerned that we were about to visit a town that was "too scary for the Gary," as Gary is legitimately one of the most dangerous delinquents you will ever meet.

We pressed ourselves flat against the stones and inched our way down the inner lip of the wall. Log and Rí took the lead. The steps are built for leprechaun feet, covered in crushed-up seashells for traction.

We finally landed at street level and it was pure chaos. North Ifreann makes Nogbottom look like Bad Aonbheannach. Little jaunting cars zipping in every direction, pulled by pigs and wild-eyed goats. Pawn shops, pickle parlors, a store that boasted WE COPY ANY SHOE PRINT!

Another sign read: CASH FOR TIN WHISTLES, NO QUESTIONS ASKED! Wee barkers were stationed outside of the dozen or so shoe stores, with stacks of lavish gold and silver shoes, heels, and buckles filling every square centimeter. The barkers sing "GET DEM CLOGS–GET DEM CLOGS–GET DEM CLOGS!" to lure in the wee folk, and this refrain becomes the soundtrack of the city.

Pickle parlors (like the very illegal Bob and Thing's in Nogbottom) are NOT illegal in North Ifreann. North Ifreann has pickle parlors on every corner with wee folk passing out coupons. In North Ifreann you can even get hot pickles delivered by haretroll right to your front door. This seems insane—but it's par for the course in this pit of a town.

Here's a sample of awful things that are entirely legal in North Ifreann:

Recreational pickletooting
The sale of and consumption of real unicorn
meat and dowsers

Bender wager dens (Leprechauns love to eat hot pickles and toot themselves into the ceiling with gas from their bottoms. In North Ifreann there are venues where you can BET on how high a leprechaun will toot into the air. This is unethical and endangers and demeans leprechauns who are already addicted to chasin' the fits. Gambling on tootin' is ALSO as addictive as the pickles, so it's a terrible cycle.)

Nonfatal stabbing (Yes, if you stab someone in North Ifreann and they survive, they have *no legal recourse against you.* This is why the town is sometimes referred to as Stabtown, Wee Pokepit, or the Devil's Pincushion.)

Shousting, which consists of leprechauns jousting in the air on flying harpies, sometimes to the death. Harpies in the shousts are sometimes fed sticky okra vindaloo to make them extra aggressive.

Lightlifting, which is the theft of "light" items. Items under three human ounces that are easily pickpocketed are fair game in the Devil's Pincushion. There is no law against stealing them; in fact, it's vaguely encouraged.

Filtherlicklims. All leprechauns like naughty poems, sure. But there's a subgenre in North Ifreann that is short for VERY FILTHY LIMERICKS. The contents of these will make a human gag or throw up instantly upon hearing them. Here's an example of one. **Do not read this unless you are somehow trying to throw up** (which is something those of us with food allergies sometimes must do).

There once was a lad from Nogbottom,
whose toots were so pungent and rotten,
they'd burn off your face,
set fire to the place—
blew his butt half a league from his coffin.

Terrible. Just terrible stuff. I hope that if you threw up it was intentional.

Within the first few seconds in North Ifreann, the fourth-ugliest leprechaun I had ever seen bit me on the knee guard and made off with my shenanogram. (This was infuriating, as detectives of the Special Unit have to pay for

replacement gear, and a new shenanogram is seventy-five euros in the S&W department.) I vowed to keep a hand on my shillelagh, and the other in a steady rotation, checking all of the items on my belt.

A block later, a wee woman with ears the size of personal pizzas tried to steal my boots. The actual boots off of my feet! She wasn't even clever about it, she just grabbed at the laces and started tugging.

"Gimme dem heels, beefie!" she howled, reeking of hot pickle and chomping a set of wooden dentures at me. I gave her a whack with my shillelagh, because sometimes violence is the answer.

The wee folk of North Ifreann are hard on the eyes. Living under a cloud of peat smoke and pickletoot fumes means Ifreannians have become distressing to look at. But North Ifreannians are also ugly on the inside, where it matters. A minute later, the wee woman was back with an accomplice and they stole the flashers off of my socks and one of my cufflinks.

"Come back, you devils!" I hollered after them, accidentally leaving my mouth open for a bucket of muck that

was dumped on me from above. (The old stone apartments in town have no indoor plumbing, so the families in them use a *muckbucket* both as a toilet and for any food scraps.)

"Thanks very *muck*, beefie!" shouted a tiny voice, making a joke that was un-hilarious from my point of view. Lots of other little voices joined in with laughter and filthy gestures.

Log pulled her shillelagh, flexing her muscles and shouting:

"[SOMETHING IN THE LANGUAGE OF THE WEE FOLK]!" She cracked her staff on the top of the meat cart, creating a huge bang.

You could hear a pin drop. The wee folk were not expecting a six-foot-tall beefie to shout at them in their native language.

Every little head turned.

"[MORE IN THE LANGUAGE OF THE WEE FOLK]," said Log with a disgusting leprechaun gesture.

The wee folk parted, giving us a wide berth. Log pulled me along and I in turn pulled Figs and Dooley. Lily and Rí held up the rear. A few leprechauns made nasty gestures at

us, such as "fall down a well" and "sit on a hedgehog," but at least nobody lightlifted us for the time being.

I saw Figs's eyes wandering toward the many pickle parlors that lined the alleyway. Some had jars of gigantic pickles in tanks filled with rocket fuel and habanero peppers. Figs licked his lips. I was deeply worried about having brought a pickle addict into the eye of the hurricane. I kept a firm hand on his shoulder, as he was back to being a little naked man.

"Now, we've got to find the kind of venue where an evil sacrifice of this sort might be happening," I said to Log.

"I know some locals who would know, but they might not be very nice to you or the hounds," said Log. "These are orthodox wee folk. Major mischief makers, hard drinkers, thieves."

"Classic leprechaun types," I said. "You can't faze me when it comes to their devilishness."

"It's just that, well—I hope you won't judge these ones too harshly," said Log, her psychotic giggle turning into a psychotic giggle of concern.

"Of course," I said, wondering why Log was being so coy.

"I hope you don't judge them harshly . . . because they're my parents."

Chapter Seventeen
LOG'S KIN

og's leprechaun parents, Dave with the Courage of a Minotaur and Mary with the Legs that Go on for Days, lived in a modest basement apartment at 723 Queen Moira Street. Their place was beneath a pawn shop called Teeth for Anything? Whether this business gives you teeth for *your items*, or you give them teeth in exchange for *their items* is not clear from the sign—and also, why the question mark?

When we arrived at Dave and Mary's wee door, I had been nonfatally stabbed six times. The stabbings were tiny and more annoying than anything, but it's disconcerting to be nonfatally stabbed so much. There ought to be a law.

Log took a pause and a deep breath at the squat front door. "I haven't seen my folks in almost three years," she said. "In truth, Ronan, I . . . um . . . this part is a bit awkward."

And then a most remarkable thing happened. A tear welled up in Log's eye. Log, the toughest human being I have ever met.

I did what she would do and squeezed her hand, hard. The wolfhounds could tell she was upset and nuzzled their bodies up close on either side of her. Wolfhounds are extremely sensitive, and will form a phalanx* around a sad human being.

"I didn't really think I would ever come back," said Log. "I love me wee mum and da, but I mostly remember them fighting. All the time. About everything. I said, 'If you keep it up, you two, I'll get you good. I'll run away and join the beefie police! Just watch me!' And I did. It took five tries, but I did just."

---

* *Okay, Ronan Boyle, you know the word phalanx, but use vendetti? I call blarney on this. Your man in a tight corner, Finbar Dowd.*

"You joined the Special Unit just to spite your parents?"

"Oh yes. They're major criminals. Me becoming a police officer was the perfect IRONIC PUNISHMENT!"

I put my arms around Log, pulling her in close. She sniffled for a moment, right into the top of my beret, certainly getting some snot on it. I love the beret, but I love Log MacDougal more, and in my mind, her tears and snot only added to the beret's sentimental value, possibly making it luckier, so it was all right.

"We can go. We'll find the captain another way," I said. "Figs must know some folks."

"No," said Log. "They must have been worried sick. And besides, this is the best part of any ironic punishment! The payoff! I can't wait to see the looks on their faces."

I remembered vaguely that I once threatened my mum and da that I would hold my breath if they didn't allow me to stay up late and watch an interview with Dame Judi Dench on RTÉ. I promptly passed out and did not get to see the interview.

Log wiped her face, dusted off her cadet uniform, and

thumped on the little door. There was a bit of cursing in the language of the faerie folk from the other side.

"'Tis yer beefie baby come home with an ironic punishment!" yelled Log. Then she repeated this in the language of the faerie folk.

It got suspiciously silent behind the door.

"They think we're thieves, trying to trick them," said Log. "Most folks who knock on yer door here in the Pincushion are thieves. Mum is puttin' on her brass knuckles right know, and Da's pulling out his fightin' mace. They'll try to jump us."

I drew my shillelagh.

"Ha. Don't worry Ronan, Mum and Da couldn't hurt a flea. 'Twas Da's twenty-seven hundredth birthday last month," said Log.

The door burst open and two ancient leprechauns wobbled out like dizzy toddlers after a carnival ride.

The male had a white beard, braided in the old leprechaun fashion with living clover. His face was as brown and wrinkled as a walnut. The female had a nutlike appearance as well, with electric red hair pinned up in buns. It was a hairstyle more suited for a wee woman in her early five hundreds (which made me think it was probably a wig).

"Oi, oh that hurts so bad!" said the wee man, trying to swing his mace at my middle, but dislocating his shoulder and falling splat on his face.

The tiny woman swung at me with a gorgeous set of brass knuckles, connecting directly with my knee protectors. The reverberation sent her right back onto her bum.

"ME TRICK HIP!" she shrieked, her wig akimbo.

Log scooped her parents up, holding them like a set of twin human babies.

"What the devil!? WHO'S THERE?" said Log's confused da. (Dave happens to be blind.) He reached out with his diminutive fingers and felt Log's famous broken nose.

"MY LOG!" said Log's da, tears spraying from his eyes.

"You probably been worried sick about me, haven't ya? Been almost three years I've been gone," said Log. "HA! I DID JUST WHAT I SAID—I JOINED THE BEEFIE POLICE!!"

There was then a remarkable lull that is hard to describe in the written word.

"What's that now? Did you go somewhere?" said Log's wee father, blinking, a dim look on his crinkled face.

"I ran away and joined the beefie police, just like I said I would. Did you not notice I was gone?" said Log, spinning to show her cadet uniform. "This was my ironic punishment to you."

"*Iconic Punch and Mints?* What's that now? Gone where? Since when? Did you bring me those socks I asked ya fer?" said Log's confused mum.

It seemed Log's parents didn't notice or remember that she had run away. This might seem odd to humans, but while three years is quite a lot to humans, to the faerie folk this might feel like barely a minute.

Log shrugged at me. She had done the Special Unit training five times—and just as a funny way to punish her parents. And they didn't even notice.

This is a major lesson: When you do something to punish someone else, take a moment to think, *who really wins?*

Whatever grudge they had, the three of them seemed to get over it rather quickly. They soon embraced in a hysterical weeping and giggling festival. The faerie folks' knack for crying is only rivaled with their talent for drinking. (Perhaps there is a correlation? One day science will tell us!)

"Ronan, Figs, Lily, Rí, may I present me mum and da: Dave with the Courage of a Minotaur, and Mary with the Legs that Go on for Days," said Log, proudly presenting her parents to us.

Little Mary beamed. She was missing most of her teeth; one gold incisor seemed to be the last remaining cast member of her gums. Each of her wee legs would be approximately the length of your neck, and I'm assuming you have a normal-sized neck.

"Get inside before ye get poked alive, beefies!" said Mary.

"Too late," I added for accuracy, feeling the sting in my various nonfatal stab wounds.

"Me little wooden daughter!" wept Dave. "I LOVE ME LOG!"

Log carried them through the squat door, folding herself down to half her normal size to do so.

I pulled Dooley after me by the handcuffs. Figs and the wolfhounds followed last.

The ceiling in the apartment was almost a meter shorter than Log, which explained her lackluster posture as an adult. But it wasn't only the low ceiling that made the basement apartment feel intimate. Log's mum was a bit of a "collector"—what humans would call a *hoarder*.

There were some trails to navigate through the stuffed apartment, between the stacks of things that dominated the rooms, floor to very low ceiling. *What's in these stacks?* you ask. Well, a few of the thousands of things I noticed: sixteen old spinning wheels, several thousand telephone books for North Ifreann and Suburbs, hundreds of boxes of shoe buckle polish, all unopened. Whole flats of Mikey Farrell's Imitation Unicorn Meat. An entire corner stacked up with harps, some missing many or all of their strings, a suit of armor about the size for an adult squirrel, thousands of old issues of *Gadfly!*, thirty or so fiddles but no bows. A full list of items would be longer than the part of my journal you have read so far.

Perching atop, or peeking out from, many of the stacks of things were cats.

Oh–so–many cats.

A quick count came to a dozen cats, at least. If something went amiss and we had to choose sides, we were outnumbered by cats. Whether these were magical cats, like the terrifying Scottish cat sìth, or just regular cats from the human realms, was as of yet undetermined. To a person with severe cat allergies, all cats can sometimes *seem* evil.

Log's folks hugged and keened for quite some time. Log made a gesture that we guests should at least *try* to join in all the weeping, as it's customary at faerie family reunions— and so we did. I did my very best, taking off my beret and burying my face in it, making convincing unhappy sounds. Log and Rí howled along. Dooley, still cuffed to my wrist, made some disapproving sounds through his pointy nose.

I wasn't sure where Figs had disappeared to. I worried that he had ditched us and ducked out to a pickle parlor, but then I noticed a cat with a hat next to me and realized that

he had shape-shifted
again. I hoped that Figs
would not stay a cat for long,
as I wanted to keep a close eye
on him, and there were already
too many cats in the room for
my comfort.

The keening and wailing from Log and her
folks continued with no end in sight. The wee folk
sometimes weep with each other for a whole day—
remember they live to be many thousands of years old,

so time management is not a big
deal for them. As a detective on
vendetti, though, time was of the
essence, and I signaled *Log, can*
we wrap this up?

"The detective and I are in a bit of a beefjif* to stop
this evil ritual, Mum," said Log, petting her mother lovingly
and adjusting her wig.

---

* Slightly negative faerie-folk term for when humans try to rush them.

I cleared my throat, not trying to be rude, but there was no time to lose and I felt like I'd been losing time for days now.

If I were to fail now, I would throw myself into the pit of fear gortas under the sewer cover on Friary Lane in Dublin.

"My captain and mentor is in the clutches of someone called Crom Cruach," I announced.

"Crom Cruach! The ancient eater of humans?" Mary shuddered.

"Um . . . I'm not familiar with the human-eating part, but he is a very icky old thing, yes. Once a mummy, now alive. While I have not seen him eat humans, he certainly has a bad reputation," I said. "It's likely that my parents unearthed him inadvertently."

The MacDougals shrieked, shaking the stacks of things. Cats and cat-form Figs scattered in every direction.

"Legend holds that Crom Cruach would eat the firstborn in the old human villages—it gave him power, and he in turn gave them protection, strong crops," said Dave. "But the wee folk who worship Crom Cruach would be at least a thousand years older than me!"

"I'm afraid they very much exist," I said. "They're called the Cult of Crom Cruach, and they're here in North Ifreann for some sort of ritual."

"Mum, Da, if ye were hosting an evil ritual here in town, where would ya do it?" asked Log of her tiny, walnut-faced parents.

"Oh, easy, on a Nonsday?"* said Dave. "No place for that but the Noggin."

"Aye, a'course," said Log, turning to me. "Noggin's what we call the Shousting Dome, as it looks just like a human skull from above."

"To this dome!" I shouted, dragging Dooley behind me. Our exit would have been more dramatic, except for the stacks of things, which required that we duck very low, form a single-file line, and exit quite slowly and carefully, so as not to be buried alive by bric-a-brac.

---

* Since the wee folk have no sense of time, all days are Nonsday to them.

Chapter Eighteen

INTO THE DOME

MOVE YER POOPERS!" bellowed Log as our bizarre entourage sped through the filthy streets of North Ifreann. Wee folk scattered away from us, toppling over themselves. From the perspective of a wee person, Log MacDougal would seem like some kind of flesh Godzilla.

Cat-shaped Figs was riding on Lily's back. Lily wasn't making a fuss about his claws in her back because she is a pro.

I raced next to Rí, still dragging Dooley along by the handcuffs, which would surely leave a red mark on my wrist for years to come. Dooley was probably complaining and making icky nose sniffs, but there was no way to hear it over the chaos of North Ifreann.

The MacDougals rode atop Rí, their tiny fists clutching his salt-and-pepper fur. Despite his blindness, Dave with the Courage of a Minotaur was calling out directions, just using his ears (a leprechaun's hearing capabilities rivals that of a dolphin).

In the hustle and bustle Mary's red wig had blown off, revealing that Log's mother is decidedly bald, which transformed her from looking *somewhat* like a walnut to being *indistinguishable* from a walnut. From a sack over her shoulder she pulled another wig. This one was platinum blond with pigtails. Why Log's mum felt the need to put on another wig at this moment will remain the greatest mystery I have ever encountered in the human or faerie realms.

We were moving so fast that I could scarcely keep track of the number of nonfatal stabbings I was getting from random wee folk—thank heavens for my Special Unit knee protectors and the Kevlar-blend jacket. I should have ditched my nice umbrella ages ago, but now I was holding on to it in my armpit like a precious totem.

The grime in the air gave my glasses a dark tint. I wiped the lenses and glanced to check if Figs was still with us. I was concerned, as we were now heading through a famous, five-way intersection of North Ifreann called Gherkin Junction—home to some of the most famous pickle parlors in Tir Na Nog.*

Figs was licking his barely existent cat lips, side-eying the pickle parlor marquees. It's likely that he hadn't had a pickle since we left the *ucky   evil*, now many human hours ago.

I could sense harpies moving about in the sooty air above our heads.

We were closing in on the Noggin. You could cook an egg on my hot pink face.

The Shoustmarket wraps around the Noggin, a half kilometer in each direction. It's in this hopeless place that the wee

---

* Queen Moira with the Magnificent Forehead exploded here, celebrating on a pickle bender on the first ever Queensday—which is named after her.

folk trade harpies (illegal), harpy saddles (made of far dar-rig fur—immoral), and lances tipped with precious stones (expensive and beautiful, worth seeing if you get the chance).

The leprechaun jockeys who ride harpies rent them-selves out by singing boastful songs about their jousting skills to potential backers. A classic jockey-rental song was being belted out as we passed a tiny man dressed in Day-Glo satin; it went something like:

> *Why not fly with wee Grant?*
> *He's a master with the lance,*
> *When it comes to riding birds, luv,*
> *He's the best ye've ever heard of,*
> *He's impossible to kill, it seems,*
> *He's won solo and on mix-coed doubles teams,*
> *And if he loses, he'll likely die,*
> *So what's to lose? He's worth a buy*
> *A thousand euros for the rental,*
> *To pass this up, you would be mental,*
> *He jousts like the devil, soars like an eagle,*
> *Rent Grant for your shoust, or he'll stab you: it's legal.*

So, so sad. The wee little man singing this looked to be at least four thousand years old. Imagine, to be *that age* and still renting yourself out in the shousts? And all because the jockeys are all under the thumb of the weegees,* who control the whole operation.

Harpy jockeys and gamblers parted at the sight of Log. A tiny man with a face like a bulldog approached us, carrying a brass shillelagh—the trademark (illegal) weapon of the weegees. He stepped right in front of Log, trying to block our path. His badge proclaimed him to be REAR COMMANDANT, SO HIGH DON'T EVEN ASK in the Wee Gaisoich (this means he was a rookie, probably in his first few weeks on the job).

"You've no business here, beefies," said the little man. "Hand me your weapons and any whiskeys or ports in your possession or I'll mail yer ears to Belfast, book rate."

---

* Of the one-thousand-euro rental fee, the weegees keep all but three euros, which goes to the jockey, who then also has to pay for his satin outfit! This is covered in the documentary on shousting made by my friend Aileen Whose Luscious Eyes Sparkle Like Ten Thousand Emeralds in the Sun. This documentary won the Grand Jury Prize in the Town of Doors film festival, which is a leprechaun film festival in Doors where most of the awards are just stolen off the table when the organizers aren't looking.

Without batting an eyelash, Log picked up the little man by his head and threw him several hundred meters. He sailed through the air for a remarkably long time. We never saw where he landed. These are the times when Log Mac-Dougal really shines. I doubt there's a human alive who can throw a leprechaun farther than my wonderful friend Log.

We pressed on through a sea of sad jockeys singing rental songs. Until we arrived at one of the vomitoria* of the Shousting Dome itself.

This particular vomitorium was sealed with a wooden portcullis thick enough to stop an elephant wearing a helmet.

A sign near the entrance read: SHOUSTING, ? P.M. UNTIL ??? P.M. This would make sense to the wee folk. All I could tell is that the venue seemed to be closed at this moment.

Log waved us back and tried to force the gate open with a deadlift. I had never seen Log fail at anything related to physical strength. Her face turned the color of my face, which was disturbing. She was lifting with her legs,

---

* *Vomitorium means "exit from a coliseum-type venue." Vomitoria is the plural form. Anyone who knows this would also know that vendetti is not the plural of vendetta. Yes, some of us ARE keeping score. Your associate in County Kerry, Finbar Dowd.*

which—while I almost never mention them—are seven times stronger than her famous arms.

It was to no avail. The portcullis barely budged a centimeter. The only thing that looked like it might break soon was Log herself.

"Stop! You'll never get in that way, you eejits," said Dooley. Except for the pain in my wrist, I had almost entirely forgotten he was with us.

"The portcullis is almost certainly beefie-proof," said Dooley. "If you keep trying to force it, you'll turn into a pile of straw."

"Mmm, complimentary straw," said Dave, to himself, welling up with tears because the wee folk love free things.

"Then how the devil are we supposed to get in?" I said, taking a slight step back from the portcullis, as I did not want to be a pile of straw right now.

"Well . . . *I* could help you. I am not your enemy, Boyle. But you would have to trust me," said Dooley, smiling like an eel at his parole hearing.

I looked to Log, who shrugged. Rí and Lily did, too (dog versions of shrugs).

"And how would you help us?" I said, with my most suspicious face and posture.

"First you have to promise that you'll leave me here in Tir Na Nog," said Dooley. "If I help you, you can't bring me back to Ireland."

"You're lying," I said. "Not a chance."

"Uncuff me and see if I'm lying," said Dooley.

This was a conundrum. If I unlocked him, he would very likely run. Could I catch him? Of course I could. I was fifteen and spry, he was basically a gargoyle with bad breath. But this would cost valuable time and I might lose the captain forever.

Against my better judgment, I took a chance.

I pulled the key from my jacket and unlocked the cuffs connecting Dooley's wrist to mine.

To my astonishment, he did not run. He rubbed the red mark on his wrist. I did, too.

"I'm going to reach into my cloak, very slowly," said Dooley, showing me his empty hand. "I have something for situations like this."

From his cloak he pulled out a key ring that held

approximately a thousand keys. Some were ancient, some were brand-new, some were stone, some looked like solid gold, some looked like lock picks a cat burglar might use.

"In my line of work, I collect a great many things. When I was your age, Ronan Boyle, I learned: *Start collecting keys*," said Dooley as he felt the squiggly edges of each key. "So many things you can collect once you have a key collection. Almost anything really. I'm surprised more people don't do it."

"If you have every kind of key, why didn't you unhandcuff yourself?" I asked, annoyed and suspicious.

"Maybe I knew you'd need me at some point," said Dooley with a strange chortle.

Ugh. He truly is the creepiest person I've ever met.

Dooley tried a half-dozen keys in the lock of the portcullis.

"Of course, it's impossible to have every key, but

eventually you'll find that there are only so many types of locks. It's probability."

I'd love to say the next key he tried opened the lock, which would be oh-so-much more dramatic, but it was actually about seventy-five keys later. (This is the kind of annoying detail I feel obligated to share with you in my journals. This is for the sake of transparency; otherwise the unbelievable things will seem commonplace.)

Key seventy-six—*Click!* The portcullis rose with a groaning of wood and metal.

"After you, Detective," sneered Dooley, tucking the key ring back into his cape.

And I ran into the vomitorium, feeling like I could boke.

Chapter Nineteen
SIOBHÁN

From the bowels of the dome I could hear the sound of dozens of harps playing a pizzicato version of a leprechaun heavy metal song.

We followed the sound until we reached the upper deck seats of the Noggin. (The most expensive seats, opposite of a human stadium, closest to the midair shousting and the violent action. The next most expensive seats in the dome are the floor area called the splatmat, where you can hear and feel the splats of the jockeys when they fall from the harpies.)

Dooley was at my elbow. We huddled in the shadows, scoping out the grand, mostly empty sporting venue.

Above us, two jockeys were swooping around on harpies, practice-jousting each other. They would circle the birds to opposite ends of the dome, then race at each other—only pulling up their lances at the last minute.

Watching them in dry runs, I could tell that shousting was ill-advised, stupid, and reckless. And remember, the jockeys are only making three euros—the cost of two Lion Bars in human Ireland.

Down below on the splatmat, a group of enchanted harps were playing the music we had heard.

A stone altar like you might find in the Burren dominated the center of the splatmat. It was circled by torches and a dozen or so free-standing stones to create a small "henge." Some of the stones were carved with Celtic symbols like the Sheela Na Gig. (A creepy image that was once kicked into my chin by the Red-Eyed Woman's shoe.)

"That altar is stolen from my shop. And the slabs,

almost this entire henge," whispered Dooley. "Two hundred thousand euros in relics that belong to me, right there, officer!"

"Hush!" I said to Dooley, as I had zero interest in his stolen henge items right now, even though a theft like that is usually precisely the work of the Special Unit.

A dozen wee folk in druid robes entered, stepping in unison. Some of the wee folk held bundles of sticks and brass cups.

Under one cloak I caught a glimpse of the bright red eyes of the Wee Woman Whose Nose Looks Like It Was Put on Upside Down. The same leprechaun who attacked me in Dooley's gallery—a high-ranking member of the weegees, and likely the ringleader of this whole cult.

Some of the wee folk played on bodhráns, pounding out an ominous tempo.

I didn't quite recognize the Bog Man, or Crom Cruach, as he was now known to me. I had only seen him as a beef-jerky mummy: once in my parents' home lab, and once in a

carriage in the rain in Duncannon Fort. Crom Cruach was now in a long black robe and hood, with only his skinless face visible. His huge black eyeballs sat in their sockets like olives. His face, mummified by four thousand years in a peat bog, had the look of a badly burnt chicken.

The wee folk began to chant:

Am chun beatha
Am chun beatha
Crom Cruach!

"We ten are gathered, the last of the devotees of Crom Cruach! We will serve him as we did in days of old. He shall protect us again! As he grows in power, so do we!" said the Red-Eyed Woman.

If I had my shenanogram it certainly would have been going haywire right now.

Log squeezed my hand, which is a lovely thing she does in frightening moments like this when my self-doubt creates a face typhoon of panic sweat, making it look like I've just stepped out of a shower.

"What's happening?" whispered blind Dave, from his perch atop Rí.

"Some dark ceremony. They're going to sacrifice Captain de Valera to this Crom Cruach, but over my dead body," I growled.

I checked the gear on my belt, which included a vast-sack* shaped like Roscommon Football Club souvenir coin purse that I'd taken from the Supply and Weapons Department. In the event of successful arrest, I'd be able to transport this entire gaggle of lowlifes back to Killarney for processing.

I drew my shillelagh, trying to calculate the best angle to attack this lot. "Now, here's my plan. Figs, Log, and I will use the element of surprise . . ." I looked around for Figs. Figs?

No.

Figs was gone.

---

* A vastsack is small on the outside, massive on the inside. This one was medium-grade; guaranteed to hold a normal-sized production of Mozart's *The Magic Flute,* which has about twenty singing roles.

"FIGS!" I screamed ever so softly, searching the shadows with my torch, in case he had changed into one of his animal forms.

Lily and Rí sniffed about. No trace of him, not even his hat.

My heart deflated. After every stupid thing we'd suffered to get here: Yum Yum, Ricky the far darrig, damp walnuts, the snakes, the hose, the on-the-lips kisses from Capitaine Hili, my brief but genuine triumph in the theater.

Figs had been virtually useless—nothing but a burden on these entire vendetti. Now he was off on a picklebender, and in our moment of crisis.

I cursed him in my head. I would write a scathing report about Figs if I ever made it back to Killarney.

My rage about Figs was soon overshadowed as my blurry eyes were drawn to the most terrifying-slash-magnificent thing I had ever seen.

Below us on the splatmat: Five weegees, each about two feet tall, ushered out my mentor, Captain Siobhán de Valera. The captain's eyes were glazed over—a symptom of the

harpy poisoning. She wasn't even in chains; the weegees were gently holding her ankles. The poison was making her a willing participant in this dreadful cult affair! *She seemed happy to be there!* Ugh. My blood boiled.

For the record: The captain was dressed in a green silk gown. The colors of the embroidery seemed to be inspired by her two different eye colors; the captain has one brown and one green eye, and the detailing reflected that dichotomy magnificently. Even from one hundred meters away, I could tell she was absolutely crushing this gown. The captain is my friend and mentor and the second-best shillelagh fighter I've ever seen. She has a brilliant mind for criminal justice, and is a steadfast officer of the Special Unit. She's everything I aspire to be as an officer and as a person. But I had never been so aware of her as, well, a human woman. It was a funny feeling like falling.

The captain is only five or six years older than me. Which is part of why she is my mentor, and THAT'S ALL THERE IS TO IT, REALLY. I don't think I have any other feelings for her, and she certainly does not for me. How

could she? I'm like a scarecrow with food allergies. Dermot Lally can't even remember my name, and for good reason, why should he? I'm only in the Special Unit because I fit into a rather small hole.

Also she's ridiculously older than me, if I hadn't mentioned that. Ridiculously so? Maybe it's just four years? I'm not really sure, as I would never ask something like that.

Many people have weird-looking feet, but the captain is not one of them.

To clarify: This is all just something I was noticing.

A detective needs to have an eye for details, and this stunning gown on the captain was the part of the details of the crime in progress that I am reporting to you. I convey these details to you with zero personal opinion, because it's unlikely that I am in love with the captain.

So, the captain was there, accounted for. I noticed her gown, for my report. *Check.* Nothing else to say on that really. *Blah blah blah*—she looked nice, for somebody under an evil spell.

The bodhráns pounded. A wee man blew a mist of

whiskey from his mouth at the torches, making them roar into giant fireballs—the most evil luau imaginable.

The captain was led up to the altar, all smiles and dead eyes. The fact that she was not fighting back was making me mental! Clearly she had been put under some sinister spell, as the REAL captain and her purple fighting stick could make seven-layer dip of this group of thugs.

Crom Cruach knelt, pulling back his hood. The Red-Eyed Woman went up on her tiptoes and put a bronze crown on his head.

"Crom Cruach! Lord of the sun! We present you this human," said the Red-Eyed Woman. "Her blood shall be spilled for you, that you might grow strong again as in days of old!"

And then I did something ever so stupid.

"Siobhán!"

I screamed out the captain's first name. This is something I never do except in my head. I screamed it as loudly as some eejit requesting a song called "Siobhán" at a rock concert. I don't think the word came from my mouth but somehow from my stomach.

Every head down on the splatmat turned to look at me. Crom Cruach locked his dead olive eyes with mine.

I stretched up to my maximum height and took off my glasses, slipping them into the Roscommon Football Club souvenir vastsack. Taking off my glasses looks like a brave move, but it is actually something I do when I'm frightened and want to have a *not so perfect* view of what's in front of me.

I adjusted my beret and twirled my shillelagh with as much menace as a Ronan Boyle type can muster.

"Listen up ye lot! I'm taking the captain and this Crom Cruach. I'm going to walk right out of here and nobody gets hurt," said somebody who sounded like me. I suppose it was me. *Must have been?* My face was beyond the red color temperature index and was moving into the light blues.

The weegees cackled, as if this were the funniest joke they'd ever heard. Crom Cruach smiled, his jerky-cheeks pulling up taut. He pulled out a bronze dagger from his robe and took Captain de Valera's hand, then he led her toward the altar.

"My lord," said the captain to Crom Cruach in a voice that was not at all what she usually sounds like. *She is*

not somebody's damsel. All of this was disgusting and out of character.

"Captain de Valera! You are not yourself right now! It's me, Detective Ronan Boyle! I've traveled a great distance to get you home!" I shouted.

When nobody reacted, I tried again. "Nobody move or you'll talk to the shillelagh!" (This is a slogan on a popular tank top that Yogi Hansra sells at her yoga workshops at Collins House, and worth a try.)

More laughter from the weegee cult. My threats weren't landing.

Captain de Valera looked up at me, her two-tone eyes blank. The real her was somewhere very far away.

Crom Cruach leaned in and kissed her. Right on the lips.

Dis. Gus. Ting. With no other plan than a whole bunch of skull cracking, I raised my shillelagh and leaped over the railing, shrieking like a madman.

"Get that beefie!" screamed the Red-Eyed Woman.

I did not land on the splatmat, as I had *sort of* planned.

Before I could hit the ground (a landing that likely

would have broken both of my legs) a harpy jockey swooped down from above and lanced me directly through my shoulder.

The confusion of being a living marshmallow on the end of a stick was compounded by the life-changing pain of the lance through the shoulder.

For some reason I noticed the useless detail that the lance had a sapphire tip, now with a tint of my blood on it.

Oh boyo did this hurt—so, so much. Tears would have streamed down my cheeks but because I was now flying on a kebab stick, the tears blew up into my eyebrows instead.

I ran my legs in the empty air like the worst pantomime of riding a bicycle that you've ever seen. The harpy jockey zoomed me up into the rafters of the dome, cackling and performing loop-the-loops, to add to my embarrassment and mental trauma.

I was crying and bleeding, and if I know me, shrieking. Kilt flapping. Other than a time I broke both wrists Roller-blading in Ayre Square, this would mark the low point of my life.

My shillelagh was gone, lost somewhere in the bleachers. And even worse: My beret was unaccounted for.

Up in the expensive seats I could make out another harpy jockey swooping toward Log, but he was very mistaken to think he could stab her through on his lance.

Log is solid muscle. The lance bounced right off her back, and the jockey and the harpy took a hard tumble into the stands. When they popped up again, Log knocked them out cold with two great swipes of her shillelagh.

Log turned and picked up her tiny parents, one in each arm. I thought it was to protect them, but that's not the lep-rechaun way.

"Ronan! Duck! I'm gonna throw me da at you!" screamed Log.

I thought I misheard her, but I did not. She took her da, wound up, and threw him directly at the jockey who was flying me about.

Dave's walnut-hard head connected with the jockey's skull, knocking him off the bird. The jockey fell a hundred meters to the floor of the dome.

I also fell. So did Dave.

Long-term planning is not Log MacDougal's strong suit.

One of the ceremonial torches broke my fall, so while

I did not die from splatting on the splatmat, I did catch on fire.

The Special Unit jacket is flame resistant, but it seems that the kilt is highly flammable. This is a dangerous detail I will report to the dull-as-paint Deputy Commissioner Finbar Dowd.

Lily and Rí leaped on top of me, rolling around, suffocating the flames with their huge bodies. I stumbled to my feet, my face steaming, kilt smoldering. I had lost my shillelagh, but I did have a huge lance at my disposal, as it was still sticking through my left shoulder and *finders keepers, losers weepers*! The fact that I was both losing and weeping at this moment seemed very appropriate.

The tears poured down my face in their proper gravitational direction.

I thought there was a chance that to pull the lance out of my shoulder would kill me, as I *feel* like I have heard that somewhere. But to leave it in would be awful as well. I took a chance and forced it out.

I did not die, but I did feel quite dizzy. The lance seemed

to hit mostly the meaty part of my shoulder, which was fortunate, as there is there is not a surplus of meaty parts on me. I ripped off a bit of the hem of my kilt and made an impromptu tourniquet for my shoulder, stuffing some extra fabric into the hole. Only adrenaline was keeping me from passing out entirely.

From the corner of my eye I saw Log wind up and throw her mum at the other harpy jockey in the air above us. With a satisfying crack, he (and Mary) bounced off the dome and dropped one hundred meters to the splatmat.

Using the lance for support, I took a step toward the altar and the captain.

Log hustled across the splatmat, scooping up her parents to use as projectiles again.

"Captain de Valera, please," I said. "Try to remember me. I am Ronan Boyle, your trainee! We must get out of here!"

The captain cocked her head, but nothing seemed to register.

"It's me, Ronan Boyle," I repeated, thinking it would jog something in her mind.

I surreptitiously began to unfasten the Roscommon Football Club vastsack from my belt. If I could buy a bit of time and get her into it, even if it meant losing Crom Cruach, it would be worth it.

Dooley was rushing around, shoving the stones and relics into a vastsack that he had brought. His sack looked like a Prada clutch from their 2020 line, sneaky devil. If his entire vendetta was to get some stolen trinkets back to his gallery—well, that is just sad. That's not even a real vendetta!

Lily and Rí fanned out and began to circle behind the weegees. (A useful tactic of the wolfhounds of the Special Unit. Two huge wolfhounds pacing behind you is so unsettling. Try it, if you have two wolfhounds.)

Then something remarkable happened: The captain gestured to the weegees to stand down, and they did. She stepped toward me, the light of the torches finding reflection in her not-quite-a-matching-set of eyes.

She smiled at me, then she spun around and kicked me in the chest, sending me flying ten meters backward.

The Red-Eyed Woman cackled and tossed the captain a brass shillelagh. The captain leaped toward me, leveling a swing at my head. I rolled away in the nick of time—a lifetime of playing "Are You There Moriarty?" with my mum and da has made me an expert at rolling away from swipes at my head.

"Captain, no! I'm on your side," I yelped. "It's Ronan Boyle!"

The captain's eyes had gone from dazed to full evil. I had never seen her look like this. I had to remind myself that this was *not* the real captain.

Log kept throwing her parents at weegees and nailed each one. Not only did Log's parents seem to not mind being used as weapons, they enjoyed it. Dave was giggling like a psychopath, as his daughter Log often does in skirmishes. If I were to tell you that this was one of the most genuine "happy family" moments I've ever witnessed, I would not be lying.

The cracking of leprechaun noggins against each other sounded like a heated Ping-Pong match.

Lily and Rí had each captured one of the downed harpies and were keeping them pinned by the napes of their necks, the best (only) way to keep a harpy subdued.

I would have said it seemed like we had the upper hand in this tussle, except for the Captain-de-Valera-versus-Ronan-Boyle part. The captain has an award on the wall of the astonishingly bad cafeteria for BEST SHILLELAGH FIGHTER 2017–2020.

If you were to make a list of people I did not want to have to fight against, Captain de Valera is in the number two spot, right after Yogi Hansra.

She came at me with a classic Hansra 1–5–3 fighting pattern that means one strike from your dominant hand, five from nondominant, then three kicks. With my proper shillelagh (that the captain herself had given me) I would have been ready for this, but with only the shousting lance, every blow from the captain connected.

A well-placed kick from the captain's not-at-all-weird-looking foot met me directly across the jaw.

This was the first time I learned that a blow to the jaw (rather than the head) is what causes a classic knockout.

I started to black out.

I could dimly see Dooley grappling with Crom Cruach, trying to get him into his Prada vastsack.

The pain in my jaw was nothing like the agony in my stomach. I had led Lord Desmond Dooley right here like some kind of hapless tour guide. Now I would likely die, and Dooley would escape with his knickknacks and my Bog Man.

I looked up at the captain and the captain's temporarily evil eyes. She was about to whack me right across the temple.

"Siobhán, wait. Siobhán de Valera, I love you," I said.

Chapter Twenty
A FRIEND

he captain's eyes blinked. *Was there a moment of recognition?* I could not say.

I have no idea why I blurted out a silly thing like what I had said. Certainly, the kick to my jaw had rattled my brain, and I was not thinking clearly. In normal situations Dame Judi would have intervened and told me what to do next.

"I mean, Captain . . . I'd love . . . to get you out of here," I sputtered, trying to think of what I must have truly meant.

"Ronan! I'm sorry, Ronan!" said Log, calling my attention over to her. The weegees had gotten the drop on the

MacDougals. Log was disarmed, and her mum and da were being held at knifepoint by the Red-Eyed Woman.

There were too many weegees for our side to get the upper hand. Lily and Rí would tip the balance, but that would mean releasing two full-grown harpies, which would be disastrous.

"Don't let the birds go!" I said, shaking my head at the wolfhounds. I looked around and did some terrible calculations. My spirit was crushed. I knew the terrible thing I had to do next. I had to admit that I had always known I was just an understudy on this mission. Filling in for some real Special Unit hero who would have had this well in hand. I dropped to my knees.

"We surrender. In the name of the Commissioner of the Special Unit, I invoke the treaty of 1979 and ask for humane handling as your prisoners," I said, putting my hand that I could lift into the air.

The Red-Eyed Woman and the weegees screamed with delight, toppling over themselves, blowing raspberries. They pulled out flasks and toasted one another. One little

man did a horrid gesture that seemed to mean "I wipe my bottom with your treaty of 1979."

And then, from below my feet, there came a low and frightening rumble.

"What is that sound?" said Log's da, who cannot see and who, with his fine-tuned hearing, was the first to hear whatever it was.

The weegees stopped laughing. Something had changed in the air around us.

Even Dooley and Crom Cruach froze, midstruggle, expensive antique daggers at each other's necks.

The weegees trembled. A shadow covered the splatmat.

I could sense something behind me. I looked over my shoulder and saw the surprise that was making everyone tremble.

A massive black bull.

He was size of a tank, well over a metric tonne (2,204 pounds). His horns were a meter long and curled to make this animal seem more like a demon than anything I've seen, including some actual demons in books.

His hoof pawed at the ground, ripping open a small

chasm below where he stood. Smoke blasted from his nostrils. He scowled and fumed, ready to charge. And atop his head, perched between his horns, was a familiar hat.

"Hello, Ronan," said bull-shaped Figs.

"Figs?!" I shrieked "Horatio Fitzmartin Dromghool? *Is that you?*"

"I told you I have frightening forms, Ronan. Nobody ever believes me, even though I mention it all the time," said Figs. "But I can't control the change-over, so I thought I'd hang back until I turned into something useful. Hedgehog-me wouldn't be much help, would he? Now let's wrap up these vendettas and get you home!"

With that, bull-form Figs charged the weegees like a runaway locomotive.

I leaped and tackled Captain de Valera, tossing the brass shillelagh to Log. Log gave the Red-Eyed Woman a magnificent Hansra Pull, sending her bottom over teakettle into a nearby pile of harpy droppings.

Overpowering the captain did little to change her spell-induced attitude. She bit me squarely on the cheek.

Bull-form Figs laid waste to every weegee in his path.

His horns bonked and poked them, sending them flying into the air like napkins.

"Log, get Crom Cruach, no matter what!" I said, tossing her the Roscommon Football Club vastsack.

I cursed myself for ever doubting Figs. The thunder of his hooves shook the dome. He deftly started to herd the weegees toward Log.

For those keeping score:

Log had my vastsack. Dooley had a Prada vastsack.

The wolfhounds had a harpy each.

Dooley and Crom Cruach held daggers at each other's necks.

Captain de Valera was pinned but biting my face, when within range.

One massive bull that turns out is our friend Figs herded the weegees.

There was no time to make a pressed sandwich, so I gave the captain one drop of Black Anvil from one of my flasks. Black Anvil is a whiskey made for the leprechaun navy that will knock out most humans and faeries. One drop is good to sedate a human for several minutes.

The captain was out. I picked her up and threw her over my shoulder before I realized that *I am not strong enough to do that.* Not at all.

I went down hard, my nice umbrella poking a second hole in my armpit. I sat for a moment, looking and feeling like an eejit. Then I took off my utility belt and used it as a strap to lift the captain. This was not part of my training, but rather a technique I once saw in a YouTube commercial about how to move furniture by yourself. A realization was washing over me. It was becoming clear that the difference between me being brave and bold, and PRETENDING TO BE BRAVE AND BOLD . . . is tiny.

From the outside, nobody could tell the difference.

Perhaps that is the secret to everything? Act like you are supposed to be there, and nobody will tell you to leave?

Act like you are brave even when you are drowning in beret sweat.

I looked around for Dame Judi but she was nowhere to be seen. I was alone.

For the first time in a long time. *Does everyone else just*

act like they're brave? I asked the hamster on the Möbius in my head. He, too, was gone. The only person left in my head seemed to be Ronan Boyle.

This was a slightly nerve-racking thought. But I vowed to myself that I would try. Try to pretend to impersonate the brave hero that I am definitely not, but could possibly convince others that I am, and *maybe what's the difference anyway?*

Rí and Lily had dragged the harpies to a holding cage, which the harpies did not like.

Bull-form Figs was herding the weegees toward Log and into the vastsack like so many rodeo clowns. Some weegees were trampled under hoof, and he would poke them up by the bottom and toss them with his horns.

Crom Cruach now had Dooley by the throat, fancy knife to his neck.

"Help me, Boyle!" said Dooley, pathetically. "I am not your enemy! Remember how I helped you?! Right? We could be mates, Boyle!"

"I'm so over this bit, *Lord* Dooley," I said.

Crom Cruach said something in (I think) Irish. He pointed his skinless finger toward the captain.

"He says give him the captain and you get to live," explained Dooley. "We'll both get to live. Just do it, boy. He needs to drink a bit o' her blood for his powers to fully come back. Don't be a party pooper!"

I'd lost both my shillelagh and the lance at this point. I had only one idea left, and it would require that I was very quick and clever—and I am often not either of those.

Crom Cruach howled. His dead eyes rolled back in their dry sockets. An electric tornado began to swirl around Crom Cruach—some manner of evil energy that seemed to be emanating from Crom Cruach himself.

"Boyle, please. He grows stronger, but he needs the captain's blood! Let him win this one. You're unarmed," Dooley helpfully pointed out. "It's over, lad."

"If he needs blood, it will be yours and mine, not the captain's," I said, inching ever closer. "And no, I don't have a weapon, all I have is this—*nice umbrella*."

I yanked my nice umbrella from where I had stashed it

ages ago. I lunged at Crom Cruach. With a crunch, the tip of my umbrella popped directly through his mummified chest. He screamed, a dry moan that burned the inside of my ears and would linger for years to come.

Out of Crom Cruach's chest poured peat, dirt, and some wriggling worms. I tried not to boke.

Crom Cruach fell to his knees, dropping both the dagger and Dooley.

The swirling energy tornado vanished. I had stunned Crom Cruach, but not killed him (which I don't think is possible anyway). But this act might be enough.

"Now, Log!" I screamed.

Log leaped in from behind, tossing Crom Cruach into the vastsack with the ease of a shoplifter stealing a Lion Bar (something Log often is in real life).

Crom Cruach was in custody!

My nice umbrella went with him, but so be it, these things happen.

I fell to my knees, as I was not yet an expert at this strap-lifting technique and the captain was very dense from Yogi Hansra's hot yoga class.

My injured shoulder was pumping in time with my pounding heart. Lily galloped over and put her warm paw on one side of the wound and Rí did the same on the other side, making a little sandwich in which I was the middle part.

The weegees and Crom Cruach were safely in my Roscommon Football club souvenir coin purse. Whatever evil they got up to in there, I did not care to know.

Log pulled some matches from her belt and burned the metal clasp at the top of the coin purse, welding it shut—now it could not be opened accidentally.

"Dooley! Hold it right there!" I said, not quite able to move from the weight of the captain and the hounds holding me up.

"Ah, yes. Master Boyle. Thanks for doing the heavy lifting. Now I shall take that sack of yours and Crom Cruach, thank you very much," said Dooley. "Crom Cruach has a date with my buyer in Dubai, and I will finally get my payment!"

Dooley jumped, his dagger aimed squarely at my face.

But it never arrived. The blade was caught mid-leap

by the bare hand of Log MacDougal. Log has *zero* problem grabbing a knife by the blade; in fact, it's something she practices, the same way you or I might practice harmonica.

Log bent the knife like a stick of gum and threw it into the bleachers. Dooley stumbled backward. He was about to pounce at me again, but he adjusted his pince-nez and got a good view of Log MacDougal looming over him.

"Good Lord, what are you anyway?" Dooley hissed.

"A leprechaun," giggled Log proudly. Then she bit him on the knee and squirted some very good mustard into his eyes. (Log carries an unmarked mustard bottle for times like these.) This was such a leprechaun move. And it was a joy to watch. I was so proud of my friend Log.

Dooley screamed, mustard dripping down his famous nose. He backed away, reaching for something inside his leather cloak.

"Get away, away!" said Dooley. "I'm warning you!"

I covered the captain's face, bracing for the worst possible scenario.

Dooley pulled out a tiny potion bottle and threw it at the

ground. It broke, but nothing remarkable happened. (Perhaps it was supposed to be a smoke bomb? From the smell, it seemed to actually be a jar of fox urine.)

"Damn those walking turnips!" yelled Dooley. "Wee devils charged me fifteen euros for that bomb!"

There was an awkward pause. Then Dooley turned and bolted away. Dooley's boots had high heels, a detail I had not noticed until right now when they *click–click–clicked* sadly across the splatmat.

Dooley disappeared into a vomitorium, his cape flapping pathetically.

"We can't let him get away!" I shrieked.

"It's all right, Ronan, he won't get very far," said Log, picking up me and the captain with very little effort, giggling like the genuine weirdo she is. "He's got a vastsack filled with relics."

"That won't slow him down," I said, tucking my own vastsack into the secure pocket inside my jacket. "That's the whole point of the vastsack."

"No, Ronan. Not the sack, it's what's in it. Dooley's in for a nasty surprise when he opens that one up," said Log with a smile.

I scanned the arena. Figs had turned back into a little naked man with a hat—he looked exhausted. The harpies were safely caged. All was well as far I could tell. Then I noticed: Dave and Mary—they were gone!

"I tossed Mum and Da into Dooley's sack when he wasn't looking," giggled Log. "Mum and Da love to travel. They love adventure. And they hate beefies. This should be quite fun."

Log giggled uncontrollably. I couldn't help but join in. Her little parents were a living tracking device in Dooley's sack. Soon I was laughing and crying along with Log. Then mostly crying. Then sobbing and laughing. Then moaning and sobbing and giggling. I was *not well*.

Lily and Rí licked my face, because they love me, and I love them back—and also because the salty taste of a human's tears are a real treat for wolfhounds. They

deserved it. I kissed Lily's ear around the bitten-off edge.

All in all, this had been a really difficult four-day weekend.

The captain was dead asleep, strapped to me like furniture that I was trying to move by myself.

"It's true," I said to the captain, "I really do."

Chapter Twenty-One
OIFIGTOWN

East (or ? on faerie-drawn maps) of Bad Aonbheannach, not too far from the Swamp of Certain Death, lies the Very Shortcut that leads to the outskirts of Oifigtown, the leprechaun capital city. Oifigtown is at the opposite end of Tir Na Nog from the Undernog; it's the wee folks' financial center, where stockpiles of shoes are kept in temperature-controlled vaults. It's also the seat of the Leprechaun Royal Family, the Leprechaun Royal Navy, and the Royal Harp and Clog Orchestra (an orchestra in which shoes and harps are the only instruments played—I've heard one of their records, and it's better than you might expect).

Per the treaties between the Special Unit and the faerie folk, I could not legally hold the weegees in my vastsack for as long as I wanted. There's a rule against this called Habeus-Nymphum. Regular faerie folk could be forcibly taken to Dublin and processed at the Joy Vaults. Weegees, however, because of their political stranglehold on faerie politics, would have to appear before King Raghnall of Tir Na Nog, or one of his Yorkshire terriers.

Per the 1979 treaty, I had twenty-four hours to present my case to the leprechaun royals, who would then decide the weegees' fate: either to send them with me to the Joy Vaults, or to the prison of the faerie folk called the Gaol. The Gaol is in the Upnog town of Doors. (The twenty-four-hours part of this treaty was added by the humans, as wee folk have no idea what twenty-four hours would be. So I didn't feel all that rushed to get any of this done.)

I stood at the bank of the River of GLOOM with the wolfhounds, Log, Figs, and Captain de Valera. The captain had awakened from her Black Anvil knockout, but was still very much afflicted with the harpy poisoning.

Figs and Rí would be bringing the captain back to Collins House, where the Mysterious Dr. Boiko would set her right. The captain's memory would be wiped, and she would not remember this whole dreadful affair.

Nor would she remember how far I came to save her. Or the silly things I might have said.

Lily and I planned to take the Very Shortcut to Oifigtown for the audience with Raghnall or one of his Yorkies, then we would return to the human Republic of Ireland with Crom Cruach and exonerate my parents. (Hopefully no time would be added to their *wrongful* sentences for *actual* prison escape. This was going to be a tricky legal matter to sort out. Also, I would have to find them, as their whereabouts were currently unknown. Also, hopefully I was not under investigation for aiding and abetting them, *which I had not*. Oh boyo, this next bit was going to be tricky indeed.)

Log was checking her shenanogram, which was pointing Upnog toward the town called Floating Lakes.

A familiar sound came from down the river. *Whoomp,*

there it is! Whoomp, there it is! The rusted, broken, and oh-so-beautiful *ucky evil* chugged around the bend toward us. The mop must have been driving, because Capitaine Hili was standing on the bow, wearing a T-shirt that said: I SUNNED MY BUNS IN BAD AONBHEANNACH. So tacky. And yet I was so happy to see her little fur body and webbed digits. She flipped around and showed her bottom "eyes" to us, laughing like a genuine nutcase.

"Roxanne Boyle! You have made your *venganges*!* Well done, *mon ami*," shouted Hili.

Hili lowered the gangplank. Rí exchanged some sniffs with Lily, then trotted onboard. Figs was about to lead the captain up, but I held them back.

"Wait," I said. I fumbled around like an eejit, patting my jacket to make sure the vastsack was still there. It was. "You're not going to remember any of this, Captain de Valera. And so . . ."

For a moment, I thought I was going to lean in and

---

* The French plural for multiple vendettas.

kiss the captain, *which would have been certifiably insane.* Of course I did not do that. She is my mentor and ranking officer and also my friend.

"You will not remember this . . ." I continued, "so I promise that I will write it all down."

I stretched up tall and saluted her. Something sparked in her and she saluted back—although I could tell that she wasn't sure why she was doing it.

Figs led the captain aboard.

Log picked me up and squeezed me, like you would do with someone you love when you forgot they were recovering from a major lance wound through the shoulder.

"Be careful, Log," I said.

"Not my style," she giggled back. "You did it, Ronan. And you thought you were the wrong boy for this mission."

"Did I say that? Out loud?" I asked, as I was well aware that this thought was on repeat inside my brain, but I keep most of my nervous thoughts to myself.

"Oh boyo, Ronan," giggled Log, "nobody knows what you're thinking better than Lara MacDougal."

"Lara! I thought we weren't supposed to say that?" I said.

"Don't—I'll break your face," she giggled. "And yes, you were the wrong boy for the mission. But somehow you ended up as the right man for it."

Log pulled a Kinder Egg from her pocket and ate the entire thing, wrapper and all, because she is wonderful and totally nuts. She put away her shenanogram and took off Upnog, along the bank of the river.

"To Ireland, Lily. By way of Oifigtown. And maybe at some point we will stop for lunch," I said, scratching Lily's chin.

Lily barked happily, spinning in a circle.

And together Lily and I trotted toward the Very Short-cut. My pink face started to fade back to its natural color of "mashed potatoes with Maldives-shaped freckles." Except for having lost my very nice umbrella for a second time, this was all wrapping up nicely.

"Yes, a brief stop in Oifigtown, then home for a game of 'Are You There Moriarty?' with Mum and Da," I said.

"I think you'll like them very much, Lily. They'll get their names cleared and their museum jobs back! I can't wait to see the looks on their faces."

This was the happiest I had been in ages. A weight was off my shoulders for the first time since I began my internship with the Galway office of the Garda almost a year ago. Maybe I wasn't just lucky? Maybe I was a real officer of the Special Unit? And a decent one at that. After all, I'd just returned a captain from one of the most dangerous places in Tir Na Nog. I let a smile take over my face for a moment, and then my mind flashed to:

Pierre the far darrig! Still a prisoner of the Free Men of the Pole! Still pinned to the wall of a hut, high in the Steps! I must go back for him. *I will go back for him!*

. . . at some later date. I put a pin in the idea for now.

ACKNOWLEDGMENTS

Love and thanks and apologies to:

Love to my human and canine family who stand by me or sit in my lap and make these books possible: Jenny, Lilo, Oliver, Pedro, and Heidi Lennon.

Apologies to my cousin Bébhinn whose glorious name was misspelled in Book 1 as Bébinn. Just for fun, it's pronounced *bay-veen*, and we are related by blood, even though she tells people that it's by marriage.

Three cheers for Ferdia Doherty, my Irishness tester from the town of Gweedore, which only exists for one day every hundred years.

Hugs to my godson, Lennon Wedren, guitarist and loyal supporter of the Garda Special Unit.

Love to my cousins the Lallys in Tuam, whose names and faces have been ever-so-slightly altered in these books to protect their identities.

Love to my parents and grandparents, the Lennons, Crowes, McSheehys, and Helms.

Love to my dream team, who are the 1995 Chicago Bulls of representation: Stephanie Rostan, Karl Austen, Peter Principato, Gregory McKnight.

To the 1995 Chicago Bulls themselves.

To John Hendrix and his amazing magical hand, the hand that PUT ST. LOUIS ON THE MAP!

Maggie Lehrman, my brilliant editor who makes these books something other than pure rawmaish. She truly is *the Shields to my Yarnell.*

And to the rest of my friends at Abrams Books:

Hallie Patterson, *the Peaches to my Herb*

Melanie Chang, *the Wind to my Earth, Fire*

Nicole Schaefer, *the Stills to my Crosby, Nash and Young and was there one other dude in that band?*

Patricia McNamara, *Maytals to my Toots and the*

Jenny Choy, *Roy to my Siegfried*

Chad. W. Beckerman, *Cheese to my Bacon Egg and Cheese on a Kaiser Roll with two ketchup packets and pepper but no salt, please*

Read on for a sneak peek
of the next book in the

Series

Chapter One
EASY STREET

In their homeland that the leprechauns call Tir Na Nog, darkness came as softly as someone flipping up your hoodie.

My partner Lily, a rust-colored wolfhound, was at my side. She shook off the last dampness of the River of Gloom, which we left in our wake. Lily is the size of a medium Shetland pony, but eight times smarter and ten times more lovable. We had passed into the Place That Smells Like Feet, which I had just named for reasons that are self-contained.

There is no sense of time in the land of the faerie folk. The wee folk just call every day "Nonsday." I looked up and saw that the sky was now full of the leprechaun constellations—as it was what we would call nighttime back in the Human Republic of Ireland.

Tir Na Nog is its own dominion with its own weather systems and even its own laws of physics. For example, in the clurichaun towns called the Floating Lakes, the gravitational pull is UP, which they have gotten used to, but makes the few humans who have been there barf, which is the non-Scottish word for *boke*.

Tir Na Nog has its own firmament of stars that has no relation to our human astrology (Orion the Hunter, the Big Dipper, and all those classics). Under the violent leprechaun's separatist Queen Moira with the World's Most Interesting Forehead, the leprechauns rearranged their constellations into shapes that that they find hilarious. The leprechaun sense of humor is depraved. Major figures in their night sky are: Unicorn Picking Its Nose, Queen Moira Ripping a Humongous Toot, and the one by which sailors in the Leprechaun Royal Navy steer their ships: Somebody's Butt with an Eyeball in the Crack, sometimes called Cyclops Eyeballbutt.

Leprechauns are the worst.

I stopped to check my bootlaces, which were a braided disaster that would remind you of those garlic bulb thingies that hang in Italian restaurants. I have never been a top-notch lace tier, and during the past few stressful days in North Ifreann I had been nervously adding knot upon knot to my Special Unit boots, which are designed to withstand the bite of a medium-power leprechaun. It would take a brain surgeon to cut me out of these laces.

Lily and I were headed towards something called The Very Short Shortcut, which leads from the Undernog all the way to the lower slopes of the Unpronounceable Volcano, which is just a few day's journey Downnog from the seat of the Leprechaun Royal Family: Oifigtown.

Safely locked inside a vastsack on my belt was a team of the weegees, the corrupt leprechaun police force, and their icky leader: the Wee Red Eyed Woman with a nose that looks like it was put on upside down. (A vastsack is a Special Unit supply that has a huge interior compartment but is tiny on the outside. This one looked like a

Roscommon Football Club souvenir coin purse.) Shoved in there with the weegees was an undead Irish god called Crom Cruach, a creepy four-thousand-year-old piece of living beef jerky, who had recently been rendered somewhat powerless by a violent boink through the heart from my very nice umbrella.

I had placed all of these devils under arrest in back in the filthy leprechaun metropolis of North Ifreann.

As a detective of the Garda Special Unit of Tir Na Nog, leprechauns and most land-based magical wee folk fall under my jurisdiction, as long as I am not violating their Republic Rights.

My current mission was to turn these corrupt wee folk over to their Leprechaun King. Ferghill, their eleven-inch-tall sovereign, resides in the royal palace in Oifigtown. I have never met a leprechaun royal (or even a human royal, except for the guy in Galway who calls himself the king of hassle-free mobile phones). Upon closing this case (which was ever so close to wrapped up!) I would then return to the Human Republic of Ireland with Crom Cruach, where he could be safely encased in the National Museum in Dublin, and perhaps the plaque beside his case would make some mention of the brave boy Ronan Boyle who brought him to justice.

My parents had been framed for the theft of the bog man by a pointy art dealer known as Lord Desmond Dooley. But they had recently escaped the Mountjoy Prison along with their prison gangs—which I had said was a bad idea at the time. My parents are museum types, but when you fall in with a prison gang like they did, you're definitely going to get peer pressured. Currently my parents' whereabouts are unknown. I don't like to use the word "escapees" but technically that is what they are right now.

Lily and I were in the home stretch! Just a quick little jaunt through this famous shortcut and, easy peasy, I'd be sitting back at Dough Bros. pizza in Galway, telling this whole affair to Delores.

Compared to the last few days, this next bit was going to be a lark! (Right!?)

Chapter 2
LAURA THE CAVE WHALE

The Very Short Shortcut is labelled on all Special Unit maps. At fifteen years old, I am the youngest person ever to hold the rank of detective in the organization, which means I get the privilege to carry one of these coveted maps and I only had to pay seventy-five euros for it, plus tax.

What's not on the map is a description of how the Shortcut works, which I was about to learn. The Shortcut is nestled in a putrid cavern, three kilometers from the River of Gloom and corkscrewing almost a kilometer into the ground. The temperature in the cave is forty-five degrees Celsius, which in Fahrenheit would be something like 113, or the hottest temperatures at which a human can briefly survive, while still getting some brain damage. No ordinary creature can live permanently under these conditions, and I assure you, the creature who lives there is far from ordinary.

The human realm has seventy-six kinds of whales with teeth. The faerie realm has three more than that. The bonus whales of the faerie realm include the Hoof-less Narwhal (a thirty ton, sea-based unicorn that feeds on whole villages of merrows in one lunch break), the Left Whale (opposite of a Right Whale, can play guitar upside-down in the style the famous human Jimi Hendrix of Seattle, Washington), and the largest and most unsightly specimen of omnivorous nonfiction whale: the Cave Whale.

We had been corkscrewing down into the cave for about a human hour, getting mild brain damage and hanging on to the sizzling stalagmites that line this nightmarish Dante set. Just when things couldn't get more unpleasant . . . we met Laura.

Laura the Cave Whale is the most inaccurately named

creature that I've crossed paths with. When I hear the word "Laura," I think of a freckle-faced girl out on the American prairie, doing chores for Ma and Pa, living her simple life by a code of friendship and love of the outdoors. Laura the Cave Whale, on the other hand, is a slug-like creature the length and girth of four London Underground train cars. She's covered in scales and gelatinous spikes, which secrete a mucus that protects her from the heat and smells like dubious Pad Thai that somebody put extra shrimp powder in without telling the recipient who might be very allergic to it.

Laura's maw is wide enough to inhale all of Manchester United (37-ish persons at this the time of my screaming). Her underbite shows off a set of rotten fangs that resembles the Tokyo skyline after a successful Mothra attack. Her eyes are huge but purely decorative, as seven hundred years in a cave has left her legally blind. Some reports say that if you linger too long in the lair of Laura, she will force you to read all of the small print on her prescription bottles.

Laura undulated herself toward us in a squishy way that

would remind anyone of a caterpillar who happened to be the size of a London Undergroud train.

"Who dares to enter the cave of Laura and ruin the vibe with their horrible aura?" bellowed the Cave Whale, inflating herself like a whoopee cushion and spraying Lily and I with a few hundred liters of hot whale mucus.

"Um. Hello, madame whale. Ronan Boyle here, come to your cave, looking for a bit of time to save." I said, wiping mucus off my neck and taking her cue and speaking in rhyme, which is considered polite in those parts of Tir Na Nog where the creatures speak. (Technically, Laura was what Special Unit handbooks would classify as monster, not creature.)

"If yer looking to make some haste, then roll in the truffle salt and let's see how you taste," said Laura, blinking her giant useless eyes and nodding toward a nearby lagoon of truffle salt that bubbled and burped like a witch's cauldron in a low-budget Halloween special.

I looked to Lily to see if she understood this exchange as I had. Lily nodded. Apparently we were to roll ourselves in this little salt lake and feed ourselves to Laura? Yech. This is why I've never liked Wednesdays.

"Just to be clear, madame, it appears we must go in your gut to use the short cut?" I stammered, trying to not let the whale mucus drip from my nose into my mouth and . . . Ugh. Fail. There it goes. It happened. Whale mucus right into my mouth.

"Indeed, narrow human, ye must get consumed, then you'll travel quite fast, through my stomach you'll pass, then launch from my blowhole right into the air, it's all a tasty and painless affair, and I should point out, for it's known near and far, if you enjoy Laura's service—please use the tip jar," said the Cave Whale, her snout wriggling a bit towards an old jar half-filled with euros, harps, and faerie gold.

I fumbled into my sporran, found a five euro note and crammed it into the jar, folding it in a way that made it seem like *two* five euro notes, a trick I learned from Dolores Mullen, my human guardian back in Galway.

Lily and I flopped around a bit in the truffle salt lake, which, to my surprise, was an absolute delight. The density of the salt makes mammals like Lily and me float on top of the lake, with a zippy feeling of weightlessness. If not for the pizza-oven temperature in the cave that was permanently damaging my brain, I would have floated on the surface there for some time, but Laura sniffed at us with her strange concave nose. She seemed pleased with our seasoning and sucked us into her mouth in a sloppy ramen-noodle slurp.

Scientists would describe the next bit as icky. We spun about in Laura's mouth while she gummed at us. She didn't use her teeth, just savored us, the same way you might keep a caramel in your mouth during the second act of musical or legitimate play. I clung to Lily for dear life. In my mind I was being dragged back to all of the bad experiences I've had in rented bouncy houses and inflatable birthday castles.

Just as I was starting to black out, a formidable

undertow pulled us down into Laura's esophagus, delivering us into something that was either her stomach and/or lungs, and then, with a rush of hot wind, we were expunged from her mucus-lined blowhole, straight up, at something like 300 kilometers per second.

TO BE CONTINUED IN

RONAN BOYLE
INTO THE STRANGEPLACE

COMING SOON!

ABOUT THE AUTHOR

THOMAS LENNON is a writer and actor from Oak Park, Illinois. He has written and appeared in many films and television shows, as well as the music video for "Weird Al" Yankovic's "Foil." This is his second novel after *Ronan Boyle and the Bridge of Riddles*.